WHOSE SIDE ARE YOU ON?

Emily Moore

— ◦◦ —

Whose Side Are You On?

— ◦◦ —

A SUNBURST BOOK

FARRAR STRAUS GIROUX

Excerpt from The Finding © *1985 by Nina Bawden
used by permission of Lothrop, Lee & Shepard Co., a
division of William Morrow & Company, Inc., and
by permission of Curtis Brown Ltd., London. Excerpt
from "A Dream Deferred" from* The Panther and the
Lash © *1967 by Langston Hughes used by permission
of Alfred A. Knopf, Inc.*

In memory of my mother,
whose love and encouragement made
many things—including this—possible

Contents

———— o o ————

WHOSE SIDE ARE YOU ON?

Report–Card Day

———— ○ ○ ————

THE CLOCK on the teacher's desk ticked away. Just fifteen minutes to go, I thought, as I shifted nervously in my seat. If only it had snowed hard enough for school to be closed, I could be anywhere else but here, sitting at my desk, waiting for my report card. I dreaded getting it because my grades for the first marking period had been lousy compared to last year. It wasn't my fault, though. Everything was so much harder in sixth grade, especially my teacher, Mrs. Stone.

The sound of jangling bracelets brought me back to the chalky smell of the classroom and to the sight of Mrs. Stone standing over my desk.

"Barbra," she said in her metallic voice, "if you're ready to join us, I'll now distribute report cards."

I gulped so loud that the kids around me heard and started giggling. Mrs. Stone shook her head and walked to the front of the room, undoing the rubber band binding the packet of report cards. She began to give them out. I sat on my hands, anxiously waiting for her to get to me. Mrs. Stone had promised that in the second marking period she was going to be even tougher than before. I didn't see how. She was hard enough on me the first time.

Several kids whooped and hollered when they opened their cards. Mrs. Stone smiled at my best friend, Claudia. She patted my other friend, Patricia, on the shoulder and said, "Nice work."

Finally it was my turn. From across the room, Claudia made an A-okay sign at me. I drew in my breath and opened the card.

Tears came to my eyes when I saw my grades. I never dreamed it would be this bad! Not one *Excellent*. In my favorite subject, reading, Mrs. Hernandez only gave me a *Satisfactory*. But that wasn't the worst of it. In math, Mrs. Stone gave me a *U*. *Unsatisfactory* is the nice word for *failed*. I couldn't believe that Mrs. Stone had actually flunked me! I felt a thump on my back and jerked around.

Nosy Kim was grinning at me. Kids called her Gumdrop because she ate a lot of candy and was fat. "Show me your report card; I'll show you mine." She stuck her report card in my face.

I pushed her hand away.

"What did you get?" she whined.

"Leave me alone, Gumdrop," I snapped.

I stuffed my report card into my schoolbag before anyone else asked to see it, and as soon as Mrs. Stone dismissed us, I took off down the block.

"Barbra, wait up!" Claudia called, walking with Patricia.

"Got to go," I called back, as if I had to get someplace fast.

Since we all lived in the River View Co-ops, I went in the opposite direction. As I ran up the snow-slicked street, my unzipped boots flapped against my legs. I didn't stop to zip them or to swipe at my tear-stained eyes. I kept running until I passed Harlem Hospital.

Out of breath, I stopped and opened the report card again. There it was—a fat, red *U*—the first one of my life. It made me feel like a real failure. Nobody in my family had ever failed at anything before. I couldn't bring this report card home. What was I going to do?

Then I saw the solution to my problem: a trash can on the corner. The sign tacked on it said *Throw It Here*. So I did. A feeling of lightness came over me. I twirled around, holding my mouth open to catch snowflakes. The next moment, a snowball splattered against my back, making me stumble forward. "Hey!" I said out loud, and looked around to see who threw it.

The street was empty except for a woman in a fur

coat hurrying along and two old men talking in the doorway of Patricia's father's barbershop on 138th Street. I was sure it couldn't have been any of them. Then I saw the real culprit peer up from behind a car and duck down again. I should have known.

"What's the big idea, T.J.?" I yelled, marching over to him.

T.J. was tall, with gleaming black eyes and deep, round dimples. Even though he was twelve, a year older than me, he was in Mrs. Stone's class, too. A long time ago, he told me that the reason he got left back in first grade was that his teacher said he wasn't mature enough to be promoted to second grade. She was probably right.

He opened his mouth wide, pretending to be astonished.

"Don't play innocent," I said. "You hit me."

"You're hallucinating."

"Then why were you trying to hide?"

"I dropped some money." He poked around in the snow. I could tell it was all a big act by the way he kept looking up, grinning that sneaky, crooked grin of his.

"Why weren't you in school today?" I asked.

"Playing hookey," he said sarcastically.

"Seriously."

He took an Oreo cookie from his pocket, waved it in my face, then popped it into his mouth whole. I walked away, disgusted.

"If you must know," he said, tagging after me, "I was getting Pop's asthma medicine and the newspaper." Pop was his grandfather, whom he lived with.

"All day?" Not that I was complaining. In school I sat next to him. It was a relief that he was absent and could not pester me, for a change.

He hitched his old green knapsack on his shoulders, ignoring my question. "Weren't we supposed to get report cards?" he asked.

"What of it?"

"How did you do?"

"Why does everybody care how I did?"

He made tsk-tsking noises. "That bad, huh?"

"Good as yours, I bet."

He stuck out his pinky and thumb. I knew better than to bet with T.J. He'd always done well in school. He never failed math or anything else. He may have been immature, but he certainly was smart.

Turning up my nose at him, I glanced away and saw a garbage truck stop in front of the trash can. A second later, I realized the terrible thing that was about to happen. I had to get that report card back before it got dumped in the trash for real.

"Stop!" I shouted.

"I'm not doing anything," T.J. said.

I waved him off and ran back to the trash can. "Wait! Stop," I called again, but the sanitation man paid no attention. He picked up the can and shook

7

the contents into the garbage chute in the back of the truck. He climbed inside the cab. The driver put the truck into gear. The truck rumbled away and disappeared around the corner. My report card was on its way to the city dump.

What had I been thinking? My mother was going to be mad enough about my grades, let alone a thrown-away report card. I stamped my foot and kicked over the can. Without a word, T.J. righted it and gave me a strange look.

"Well, I know you're dying to ask me what's wrong," I said.

"Here," he said, offering me a cookie from his pocket.

"No, thanks." I loved Oreos, but I didn't trust T.J. The last time he offered me ice cream, it was a Dixie cup filled with mushed-up peas and mashed potatoes. Besides, I was in no mood to eat now. I sniffed and crossed the street.

He kept walking with me toward my building on Harlem River Drive. The River View Co-ops took up the entire square block from 139th to 140th Streets and from Fifth Avenue to the Drive. The buildings were red and beige brick and were built around an inner courtyard. I lived in building number 4, which faced the Drive and the East River. From halfway down the block, I heard the swishing sound of traffic on the Drive.

"Come on, take it," he said gently. "It will make you feel better."

"Nothing could make me feel better." But the thought of the bittersweet chocolate and sweet, creamy center made my mouth water. "Okay," I finally said. "I'll take one, thanks."

I bit into the cookie and almost broke my tooth. It wasn't a cookie at all, but a wooden disk made to look like one. T.J. bent over, laughing.

I threw the fake cookie at him and pushed through the doors of my building's lobby. "I hate you, Anthony Jordan Brodie!" I'd never fall for one of his tricks again.

"Can't you take a joke?" he called after me.

I turned around, sticking my tongue between my teeth, and gave him a loud, sloppy raspberry.

Wishful Thinking

———— o o ————

I DUMPED my books on the kitchen counter and poured myself a glass of ice-cold chocolate milk, hoping it would make the burning in my stomach go away. It only gave me the chills. I stomped upstairs to where our bedrooms were. All the second-floor apartments in our co-op were duplexes.

The door to my brother Billy's room was slightly opened. His baseball and swimming trophies were lined up on his dresser, along with his comb, brush, and cologne bottle in the shape of a steam engine. He loved trains. The Tyco train set he'd received for Christmas took up much of the floor space in his room. Pushing the door open a bit more, I could see the brown report-card envelope leaning up against his mirror like another trophy on display.

"Hey," he said, glancing up from his homework. "What took you so long to get home?"

"I bumped into you-know-who. The pain." I told

him about T.J.'s trick and finished by saying, "I felt like smashing his face in the snow."

But Billy only laughed. "He likes you. That's what grownups always say about kids teasing each other."

"They sure don't know anything about me and T.J."

"If you say so," he said and reached into the old, battered briefcase that had belonged to Daddy when he was a reporter. Daddy died in a plane crash when we were four years old. Billy's named after him.

Billy pulled his protractor out of the briefcase. He carefully measured angles and made calculations. While I was still struggling with division and word problems, he was doing geometry. It was hard to believe we were twins. I was ten minutes older; he was ten times smarter—which is why I was in a regular sixth-grade class and he was in the IGC, the class for "intellectually gifted children."

I pushed aside his blue plaid curtains. The snow continued to fall thick and steady. How I hoped school would be closed tomorrow. Hmmph! Fat chance! I let the curtain fall back in place and went to my own room. After changing into old jeans, I got out my schoolbooks and worked on my homework until it was almost dinnertime.

Passing Billy's room on my way downstairs, I heard his trains chugging around the track. He'd be in for it when Ma saw he hadn't set the table. But as I

11

entered the kitchen, I was surprised to see the yellow dishes on top of the daisy-patterned place mats. Billy had even made a tossed salad. Everything was ready for when Ma came home in a few minutes. Now I would be the only one she'd scold.

When I heard her at the door, I figured it was best to try to be extra nice. I kissed her hello and helped her off with her coat. "Let me take that," I said, putting her briefcase on the lacquered Parsons table next to the coat closet.

"My, what did I do to get such treatment?" She pulled off her hat and ran her fingers through her short, curly hair.

"You work hard, and I'm sure you're tired."

She sank down on the sofa. "It's worth it." I put her boots in the bathroom to dry.

She sat with her eyes closed for a while, then got up and stretched. "After I change, I'll warm up the leftover turkey and gravy for sandwiches."

However, instead of going up to her room, she went into Billy's. I tried to hear what they were saying, but the sound of the trains drowned out their voices. All I could do was hope for two things—that Ma did not notice the brown envelope on Billy's dresser and that Billy didn't start blabbing.

In any case, report cards would have to come up during supper, the time when important family discussions took place. Usually, the first thing Ma

12

did once we sat down to eat was to ask us about school. But tonight she started telling us about what happened to her at Citibank, where she is a manager.

"I got a promotion," she said. "It's now official. I'm a vice president."

"Wow!" Billy said. "That's just one step from president."

"It's many steps away, but it's exactly what I've been working toward. It will mean longer hours," she said and then gave us some other details about her new job.

"More money, too?" Billy asked.

She nodded. "Most definitely."

"Oh, Ma, that reminds me," said Billy.

I knew he was going to tell her about his report card. In the excitement of Ma's news, I had almost forgotten about it. My heart began to beat faster.

"Ma," Billy said, "I'm going to need a new baseball uniform. My old one is too small."

"No problem," Ma said, then faced me. "Are you all right? You're awfully quiet."

"I'm okay."

"You sure?" Ma ate a forkful of salad.

"Uh-huh." I pushed my plate to one side. All this suspense took away my appetite.

"Is something wrong with your food?" Ma asked.

"Big lunch," I said, getting up from the table.

"It's almost eight hours since lunch."

"I ate a big snack, too."

Ma told me to sit back down. "You know the rules. We eat as a family."

Rules, rules. Rules made me sick. I propped my elbows on the table, but one look from Ma and I began to eat slowly. Billy was cutting his sandwich into bite-size pieces. Whoever heard of eating a sandwich with a knife and fork, even if it was a sloppy kind of sandwich? Everything about him was so proper and right. He would never even *think* of throwing away his report card, let alone do it.

"Can I go upstairs now?" I asked after forcing down the last of my turkey sandwich.

Ma put her hand to my forehead. "What's the matter?"

"Nothing."

"You call T.J. nothing?" asked Billy, with a silly grin on his face.

"He's such a pain," I said, grateful to him for changing the subject.

"The way you and T.J. needle each other," Ma said, shaking her head. "It's . . ."

"It's his fault," I said, cutting her off. "Like when he put that caterpillar down my back."

"That was last summer at the Labor Day picnic," said Billy, as if a few months made a difference.

14

"And the caterpillar was made from a pipe cleaner and yarn."

"It wiggled like it was real. I thought I was going to die."

"Oh, Barbra," Ma said. "You're exaggerating."

"He's always bugging me, Ma."

"You know what they say." Billy was hinting again about T.J. liking me. I kicked at him under the table.

Ma ate some more salad. "Anyway, I've invited his grandfather and him to dinner Friday night," Ma said.

I nearly jumped out of my seat. "Oh, no. You didn't!"

"Since T.J.'s mom is still away, it's probably lonely for him."

"So what," I blurted out.

She gave me a look and I knew I had said the wrong thing. So I quickly said, "I don't feel well. May I be excused?"

Ma drew in a long sigh. "Go on."

I ran up the stairs to my room, shut the door, and got ready for bed, even though it was way before my bedtime. Going to sleep was the only way out of my mess. Why, oh, why did I ever do such a stupid thing?

I hugged Brown Bear close until he was all squished up. Ever since I was a little girl, hugging

15

him always comforted me. Just as I was falling asleep, I heard the click of my door.

Ma came into the room. She stood over me a long time before sitting down on the edge of my bed. When she turned on the lamp, my eyelids fluttered, but I kept my eyes squeezed shut.

Brushing down my bangs, she said, "Whatever is bothering you, you can tell me. I'll understand."

I looked up at her. This is silly, I thought. Sooner or later she's going to find out. I should just get it over with. I sat up and finally told her about how Mrs. Stone failed me in math.

"No wonder you're upset. But, honey, I'll see that you get help. And I suspect it's not as bad as you make out."

"It's worse."

"Let me see." She held out her hand.

I looked down. "You can't." Twisting the blanket around, I said, "See, there was this trash can, and a sign. Then T.J. hit me with a snowball and I forgot all about it. Then a garbage truck came . . ."

"Talk plainly, Barbra."

"I threw my report card in a trash can."

She didn't say anything.

"I tried to get it back," I rushed on to explain, "but I was too late. The garbage man wouldn't listen."

She sat there, not saying a word. The change in her expression was like what happened to that Dr.

Jekyll in the movie. One minute he looked like a regular person and then the next he looked real mean and evil.

"How could you do such a thing?" she said in such a quiet voice I got goose pimples.

"It was an accident. I never meant to throw it away. Not really. But that T.J. . . ."

"Don't blame him," she said.

While my voice was high and shrieky, Ma stayed quietly angry.

"In a way, it's kind of funny. Don't you think?" I looked at her hopefully, but she was not amused.

"It wasn't on purpose!" I said.

"Wasn't it?" she asked. "You never think. And now look what's happened."

"I was so upset. I never got a *U* before, and I was scared of what you would say."

"I'm disappointed in you." She got up and left. I threw Brown Bear across the room. He could stay in that corner forever.

After a while, Ma came back into the room with a long, white envelope in her hand. She laid it on the dresser. "Give this to Mrs. Stone. She'll write you another report card, and I'll talk to her tomorrow at the parent-teacher's conference." She saw Brown Bear in the corner, picked him up, and put him on my chair. "You're grounded. You won't have any special privileges."

17

"Forever?" I asked in a panic.

"Let me finish. No special privileges until your math grades improve."

That may as well be forever, I thought, as she closed the door behind her.

Good News and Bad

———— o o ————

FIRST THING the next morning, Mrs. Stone asked for the signed report cards. I pulled Ma's letter halfway out of my schoolbag, but I didn't have the nerve to give it to her in front of the whole class.

"Do I have them all?" Mrs. Stone asked, waving the packet in the air. I wondered if she could feel that one was missing. Sometime later, in private, I would give the letter to her. Until then, I would just act normally. I put my homework on my desk to be collected, then went to sharpen my pencils. On my way back to my seat, I noticed the envelope on the floor. It must have fallen from my schoolbag. Before I could get it, Kim picked it up.

"Give me that," I said, reaching for the envelope.

She hid it behind her back, all the while chomping on something—a gooey gumdrop, no doubt. "Mrs. Stone's name is written on it."

"It's mine."

Kim bit her lip as if thinking it over. Meanwhile, Mrs. Stone noticed. "Kim, bring that up here."

If Mrs. Stone read that letter aloud, I'd be the laughingstock of the whole, entire sixth grade. And all because of Gumdrop. I'd fix her but good. I stuck my foot out into the aisle, but she stepped over it without tripping.

"Thank you, Kim." Mrs. Stone opened the envelope. "And empty your mouth," she added, not even looking at Kim as she spat a wad of gum into the trash can.

Over the rim of her glasses, Mrs. Stone glanced at me as she read the letter. After she finished, she called me to her desk.

"Why do you need another report card?" Mrs. Stone asked in a low voice.

"The letter explains it."

She showed me the letter. Ma requested another report card without any explanation. How could she have done this to me?

"Well, Barbra," Mrs. Stone said. Her head bobbed, showing her impatience.

"I lost it." I swallowed and went on. "I, um, reached into my schoolbag to give it to my mother, you know, um, to sign. And it wasn't there."

She gave me a long, hard look to see if I was really telling the truth. "Why wasn't it in your schoolbag?"

"It was, but . . ." I shifted uneasily, then asked, "Will you give me another one?"

The bell rang for first period and Mrs. Stone said, "Barbra will stay behind. The rest of you may go to your reading classes." She went into the hall to ask her reading group to wait outside.

On her way out with Patricia, Claudia whispered, "We'll wait by the water fountain."

The last person to leave was T.J. At the door, he brushed his two pointer fingers together and said, "Shame, shame."

I threw an ink eraser at him just as Mrs. Stone was coming back. She scolded me, then made me pick it up.

"Do you have a problem, Anthony?" Mrs. Stone asked T.J.

"No, ma'am," he said and hiked out of the room fast.

I knew what Mrs. Stone was going to say—I'd heard it before. "You have to try harder. Don't say you can't." And that's just what she said, adding, "Until you change your attitude, you will continue to do poorly. Losing your report card is an example of your carelessness." With that, she slipped Ma's letter into her roll book and told me to go to reading.

By now, only a few kids were straggling through the hall, but as they promised, Claudia and Patricia were waiting by the water fountain. I hurried to meet them.

Ever since this past summer when Patricia moved into River View, she, Claudia, and I were together every chance we got. Claudia was the lucky one, because she and Patricia both lived in building number 6 and went to the same ballet school. Ma refused to pay for lessons for me on account of what happened last year. She had signed me up and after three lessons I begged her to let me stop. Even though I promised not to drop out this time, she wouldn't let me take them.

"What did Mrs. Stone say?" asked Patricia.

"Gave me a lecture. I lost my report card," I said, trying to sound nonchalant.

"Anybody can lose a report card," said Claudia.

"True," I said and crossed my fingers, hoping they would never find out about the dumb thing I had done. Lately, they seemed more grown up than me. Patricia put berry-stained lip gloss on her lips, then passed it to Claudia. Even though I wasn't allowed to wear makeup yet, I spread the lip gloss on with my finger anyway. I didn't want Patricia thinking I was a baby or something. My lips felt as if they were coated with perfumy grease.

Patricia capped the tube and tossed it into her shoulder bag. "I have something important to tell you."

A teacher looked in the hallway and said, "Move along, girls, before the bell rings."

"Tell us quick," said Claudia.

"Lunchtime."

"Pass me a note later?" I asked.

"And get old Stone-face mad?" Patricia bobbed her head, mimicking Mrs. Stone. The three of us laughed and hurried off to our rooms.

When I got to reading, Kim was doing my job of giving out the skill books. I snatched them from her.

"Mrs. Hernandez told me to give them out, and Mrs. Stone made me give her the letter," she said.

Without a word, I brushed past her and finished giving out the books. Afterwards, I took my seat, which was across the room from Gumdrop Kim, thank goodness.

At lunchtime, when I saw the hot lunch of ravioli and mushy green beans, I just got a milk and an apple, then went to my class's table. The boys were crowded at one end, the girls on the other. Patricia slid over to make room and gave me half of her tuna sandwich. Claudia shared her Ring Dings. Kim sat down across from us. When she bit into her sandwich, jelly dripped down her blouse. She wiped it off and stuck her finger in her mouth. Angie and Felicia giggled.

"Pig," said Patricia.

Claudia howled with laughter. I made a face at Kim, still angry about this morning. Kim's eyes got sad and droopy. No wonder nobody likes her. Not only did she make trouble, she wanted pity besides.

Patricia elbowed me and we went out into the schoolyard. Little kids climbed to the top of the snow piles. To get them down, the yard teacher kept blowing his whistle. We sat on the steps away from the noise, Patricia in between Claudia and me.

"My mom is letting me have a birthday slumber party this year," Patricia finally announced.

"No lie?" cried Claudia. We both squealed with excitement.

"Pajamas! I have to get new ones," I said.

"Me, too!" Claudia and Patricia said at the same time.

"When is it? I can't wait," said Claudia.

"My birthday, dummy," she said, with a roll of her eyes. "Weeks from now—April 5."

I asked, "Who else is coming?"

"So far, I've only invited you two, my best friends." She put her arms around our shoulders. "And I want you to help me plan the menu and pick out the videos."

"Videos, too?" Claudia and I said together. We all laughed. We were like triplets, saying the same things at once.

"You can even help with the invitations. The morning after the party, my mother is taking us out to breakfast. No places around here either. We're going to 'I Hop.' "

I didn't know what "I Hop" was, but it sounded

like someplace special. "It's going to be the best party ever," I said, wishing it could be tonight.

We were so excited about the party we talked about it after school. Patricia has three-way dialing and called Claudia and me at the same time. I was still on the telephone when Ma came home from the parent-teacher's conference. She didn't look too happy. I hung up fast.

"Hi, Ma," Billy said, without looking up from the television program he was watching. "Did you see my teacher?"

"And everything is hunky-dory and hotsy-totsy," I blurted out and regretted it at once. It sounded as if I was jealous, when really I was mostly nervous.

Ma ignored my outburst. She told Billy how pleased his teacher was with his progress, then said, "Watch TV up in my room, so Barbra and I can talk."

"Sure, Ma."

For Ma to send Billy out of the room, I knew this had to be serious.

She sat down on the couch and motioned me to sit next to her. "We had a long talk, Mrs. Stone and I," Ma began. "We both agree math isn't the whole problem."

"I told you so," I said, glancing up at her.

She went on to say, "The problem is, you don't try hard enough."

"I do so try."

"Also, whenever Mrs. Stone teaches a new idea, you fall apart if you don't understand it right away, especially division and word problems."

"See, that proves she doesn't like me," I said. "You don't fail somebody because they don't understand those dumb word problems."

"That's what a failing grade means—you're having trouble understanding. I think it's better to fail now when there's time to do something about it."

"Do you know she passed Greg and he's a real knucklehead?"

Taking my hands in hers, she said, "I know how you feel. Honest, I do."

"Did any teacher ever fail you?" I sniffed.

"Look, I know failing makes you feel bad. But it's not the end of the world. You did pass the first marking period, and there's no reason why you can't pass the last one—with some help."

"What do you mean?"

"We think a little push in the right direction is all you need. Mrs. Stone and I decided the peer-tutoring program would be a good idea."

"What?"

Without a word, she bent over to unzip her boots.

"No, Ma."

"It's already settled. And remember, no special privileges until your math grades improve."

"Patricia's giving a slumber party next month," I said cautiously. "She invited me, and I already said I'd come."

"If your math grades have improved by then."

"But—"

She gave me a sidelong glance as she placed her boots beside her seat. "The rule still stands."

"What about school trips? And suppose I want to do homework with my friends?"

She thought for a moment, then said, "Okay. Here's a fair compromise. The only restriction I'll put on you is the slumber party."

"But that's the only thing I want to do. Can't you . . ."

It was no use. I could tell by the set of her mouth that pleading was a waste of time. I got to my feet. "What's the difference if I can do word problems or not? Nobody ever has to solve junk like that in real life."

"I do," she said flatly.

Then it occurred to me what a stupid thing I'd said. She used math all the time at her job. "I don't want to work for a bank like you. I'm going to do something where I'll never think about math again."

"One day you'll have to balance your checkbook, keep a budget."

"I'll use calculators, just like you."

She shook her head. "And when the calculator breaks down. What then?"

"I'll get it fixed," I said. "Besides, even when I understand the classwork, I forget everything later. I make mistakes and don't know why."

"That's why you're getting tutoring help," Ma said.

"Everybody'll think I'm a dumb bunny."

"Oh, come on."

"It's true."

Ma called Billy downstairs and asked, "How's that girl doing that you tutor in math?"

He stood on the stairs. "Great! On her last test, she got a ninety."

"And I bet she gives up all her free time, too," I said.

"But she got a ninety, Barbra," Ma said, proud of a girl she didn't even know.

"It's March already. What good will tutoring do now?" I asked.

"A push. Remember? That's all you need."

"I don't want those snobby IGC kids telling me what to do."

Billy said, "They're not snobs, and not all the tutors are in IGC either."

"I won't do it. I'll stay in sixth grade forever."

"Your choice," Ma said, taking *Essence* magazine from the coffee table. "But if Patricia's party is important to you, you'll work hard to get better grades." She sounded like Mrs. Stone.

"That's not fair."

"That's how it is." She flipped through the magazine. "Take it or leave it."

Without a word, I stormed upstairs to my room and threw myself over the bed. I would die if I missed that party. Just die.

My Tutor

———— o o ————

CLAUDIA SUCKED ON her braces. "Maybe you'll get someone cute."

"It probably won't even be a boy," said Patricia.

"I don't care," I said, making a hero sandwich from meatballs and Italian bread, "so long as I get it over with."

"You don't mind getting stuck with one of those creepy IGC kids?" Patricia asked.

I almost said that one of those creeps was my brother, but Claudia reminded Patricia of that. "But they won't dare make your own brother your tutor. That would be embarrassing."

"He teaches a girl," I said, "in the dumb class."

"I would flat out refuse," Patricia said. "Tutoring, I mean."

"And flunk math for the year?" I took a bite of my hero. It was delicious. The lunchroom should have meatballs every day, not just Fridays.

"Go to summer school," Claudia said. "I went for reading, summer before last. Remember?" And she cried when our fourth-grade teacher told her she had to go. I suppose she wanted to forget that part.

"I'd rather do it now than in the summer." To keep from sounding like a baby, I didn't tell them about my punishment.

"You act like you want tutoring," Patricia said.

I sipped my milk and thought about how confused I was feeling. Part of me certainly did not want some know-it-all kid telling me what to do. But another part of me wanted to pass math, not just so I could go to the slumber party, but because deep down I really wanted a good report card.

Patricia pointed to Kim, who was getting up from the lunch table. Her flimsy skirt had risen halfway up her thighs, and she hadn't noticed.

"You'd think she'd feel the air on those fat legs of hers," Patricia said. Loud enough for the boys to hear, she added, "Now suppose you get stuck with *that* tutoring you?"

When Patricia said that, I nearly choked on a meatball. "That's not funny," I said.

All the boys started jumping up and down, hooting. Except for one. T.J. He stood up to see what everyone was laughing at, then shook his head. For some reason, the way he acted made me feel that laughing was wrong. Without a word to any of his

31

friends, he walked over to Kim and whispered something into her ear. She quickly pulled her skirt down, dumped the tray into the trash can, and ran out, bumping into kids.

"You girls!" T.J. said, standing over us.

Patricia waved him off and sipped her milk, making a slurping noise.

"You're the worst one," he said to her.

"Who, me?"

"Yeah, you."

Patricia stood up. "You got nerve. Trying to be a goody-goody."

Everyone at the table became silent. I thought about a day two months ago. Mrs. Stone was absent, and we had a substitute teacher. Patricia kept talking during the language-arts lesson. T.J. yelled at her to shut up, and Patricia told him to mind his business. "Make me," he said. "I don't make monkeys," she said, twisting her shoulders back and forth. "I train them." The class roared. The teacher banged the ruler against the edge of the desk and, instead of scolding both of them, she yelled at T.J. to go to the assistant principal's office.

"Hey, she started it," T.J. said.

"Don't talk back," the teacher said. "Now go to the office."

"But I didn't do anything."

"To the office!"

T.J. got up, collected his books and jacket, and

stormed out of school. The next day, his grandfather had to talk with the assistant principal, Mr. Martinez, before T.J. could come back.

Patricia and T.J. now glared at each other, neither one moving. Patricia put her hands on her hips. "What are you going to do, Mr. Big Shot? Beat me up?"

"I don't pick fights with girls," he said and walked off. His friends, Randy and Greg, followed him. Patricia made a nasty gesture with her finger, then sat back down.

I let out my breath. "Why did you say those things?"

Patricia fussed with her bright purple hair clip. "He should mind his own business. He started it. Not me." She looked to me to agree with her.

It was impossible to discuss anything with Patricia when she got an idea into her head. So all I said was, "I forgot how this whole thing started, anyway."

"We were saying how awful it would be if Gumdrop became your tutor," said Claudia.

That afternoon, Mrs. Stone handed me a slip of paper. "Here's your tutoring assignment and schedule," she said.

Walking back to my seat, I opened it, then stopped. I could not believe what I was reading. I went back to Mrs. Stone's desk.

"There's a mistake," I said.

33

She glanced at the paper and read out loud, "Tutor: Anthony. Pupil: Barbra. Time: Monday and Thursday at lunchtime. Place: library. No, it's right."

"Can I have someone else?"

"*May* I have someone else," she corrected me.

"May I?"

"No. The tutors have already been assigned. Besides, Anthony is the best math student in the class."

"We don't get along."

"You and Anthony have been in the same class since first grade."

"And I've always hated it. Please, Mrs. Stone."

She motioned me to return to my seat. "We'll be finishing our black-history studies next month," she said to the class. "As a culminating activity, each person will choose a topic on which to report."

I sat back down. T.J.'s head was buried in his book, but he had that sneaky grin on his face. I wondered how he got Mrs. Stone to let him be my tutor.

"Black-history month was over in February," Randy said.

"But our studies are not, and don't call out," said Mrs. Stone. While she talked, I wrote T.J. a note: "What are you up to? You got Mrs. Stone to let you be my tutor. Right?"

In capital letters he wrote: "WRONG."

34

After school, on our way outside, I grabbed T.J.'s jacket sleeve. He slapped at my hand like I was a mosquito. I pushed him, but he just laughed.

"What's so funny?" Randy asked.

T.J. nodded toward me. Randy looked me up and down with his bug eyes, then said, "She is kind of funny, at that."

I stomped T.J.'s foot so hard he yelped and hopped down to the sidewalk. Claudia, Patricia, and I cracked up.

"Let's deck her," said Greg, shaking his fist at me.

"That's okay. I'll get even with her." T.J.'s eyes gleamed.

"Wanna bet?" I asked and strode off with my friends.

I kept my fingers crossed that his toe was hurt so bad he wouldn't be able to come to dinner. But at six o'clock the doorbell rang. T.J. stood in the doorway, looking sheepish in front of Ma. He held his cap in his hands and called her "ma'am."

"I'm sorry your grandfather couldn't come," Ma said.

"He said he didn't feel like climbing down five flights of stairs, then back up again."

Ma smiled at that. I thought it was rude of Mr. Treadwell.

"You can take a plate of food to him," she said and then handed me T.J.'s jacket to hang up. I held it by the tag with two fingers as if it were contaminated. T.J. put his knapsack on the Parsons table.

After Billy showed T.J. his new engine, we all went to the kitchen. On the table were platters of juicy barbecued spareribs and chicken, a bowl of potato salad, and green bean salad.

"This is great," said T.J. "Like a picnic."

"Yeah," I said, passing the spare ribs to T.J. "I wish I had a caterpillar for you."

As he bit into a sparerib he looked at me as though he didn't remember what he'd done to me last Labor Day.

For a while, we ate quietly. Then Ma finally asked T.J. if he'd heard from his mother.

"Yes. She's doing real well, too. She works in a restaurant in the daytime and in a nightclub at night. She even sent me some tapes." He looked at Ma expectantly.

"We'd love to hear them," she said. "With dessert."

I groaned. Was his idea of getting even to make me sit through his mother's boring singing?

After dinner, I plopped down in a chair and picked the nuts from my butter-pecan ice cream.

"She's the best," T.J. said while Ma put on the tape. "Wait and see."

At least, when the music came on, he stopped bragging. His mother had a soft, throaty voice. I'd forgotten how good she was. Even in church, people used to applaud her when she sang in the choir. The song she was singing on the tape was like Gospel jazzed up. It made me want to bounce and snap my fingers.

"Everyone always said Irene was going to be another Billie Holiday," Ma said. She and T.J.'s mother were childhood friends. They even grew up in the same building.

"She'll be bigger," T.J. said.

By the end of the song, I was hugging the sofa cushion, swaying. What happened in school seemed like such a long time ago.

"Listen to this next one," he said, gesturing like a conductor while his mother's voice went real deep, then high like a soprano, and trilled.

"Wow," said Billy when it was over. "I want her autograph for my collection."

"Sure," said T.J. "I'll ask her the next time I write to her." He picked up his dish of ice cream, which had melted.

"I'll get you some more," Ma said.

"I like it melted," he said and turned the bowl up to his mouth to sip it.

I giggled, but he paid no attention.

Billy asked, "When do you think she'll be back?"

He wiped the ice-cream mustache from his upper lip and said, "She's sending for me. And that'll be soon. Real soon."

It was two months since she left. It seemed like

soon had already come and gone, but I didn't say that. T.J. dug another tape from his knapsack, and for the next half hour the sound of Irene Treadwell's voice filled the living room as if she were right there. No wonder T.J. carried that knapsack wherever he went. He kept her tapes in it, and they were obviously very important to him.

"She sings good," I finally said, but my voice was so soft no one heard me.

T.J. never stopped talking about his mother, even while we walked him home. I'd be mad as anything if Ma went away and left me. But he talked as if leaving him was the best thing she could have done. He was sure one day she would be a big star, send for him, buy a house in California with a swimming pool, and when he grew up he would go to UCLA and surf in the Pacific Ocean. It sounded like a fairy tale to me.

We reached his stoop and T.J. thanked Ma for dinner. He turned to me and said, "Good night. Sleep tight. Don't let the bedbugs bite."

I gave him a raspberry.

"Barbra!" Ma said.

T.J. only laughed and said, "I'm used to her raspberry goodbyes."

As we walked back home, I thought how odd it was that T.J. hadn't played one trick on me. Tonight he had acted like a different human being.

38

. . .

On Sunday, T.J. went back to being a pest. We were in church. As usual, Ma was singing in the choir, and T.J. and his grandfather sat behind Billy and me. Now and then, T.J. kicked the back of my seat. Finally I turned around to complain, but his grandfather stared at me so hard I slid down in my seat and never turned around again, even though T.J. continued kicking my seat. He wasn't going to get away with that. When services were over, I intended to pay him back.

At last, everyone filed out of church, but I followed T.J. down to the Sunday school room and peeked at him from behind the glass door. In the middle of the room, T.J., Randy, and Greg started playing kung fu, kicking their legs up, making crazy hand movements and gorilla noises. They were a sight. It wasn't until I spotted Deacon Bob at the top of the stairs that I got my idea.

"What strange noises I hear," I said.

"Strange?" Deacon Bob came bustling over. He was short and had thick, bushy eyebrows that hung over his eyes like hairy veils. In the center of his head was a shiny bald spot. He rocked back and forth on his heels as he watched T.J. and his friends acting foolish.

He pushed through the door and said, "Well, well, well. You boys sure have energy to burn today."

39

Greg tucked his shirt into his pants, Randy scooped up his tie from the floor, and T.J. scrambled to put his shoes on.

Scratching his chin thoughtfully, the deacon said, "How about putting that energy to good use?"

"They can set up the table and chairs for the church supper," I suggested quickly.

"Hey, wait a minute," cried Greg.

"I got to go home," said Randy.

T.J. laid his hand on Randy's arm and said, "No sweat," while looking at me. "A little work never hurt anyone."

Before leaving, Deacon Bob said to the boys, "I'll check on you later." He faced me and winked.

I winked back. It felt good, playing a trick on T.J. But that night I realized tutoring was going to start the next day. T.J. could give me all the wrong answers. Because of him, I might miss Patricia's party and fail math again. Then the joke would be on *me*.

Problems, Problems

——— o o ———

NOT ONCE did T.J. mention math tutoring. He didn't even stick his crumpled-up papers into my desk as he usually did. It was like waiting for the part in the movie that scared you—wanting it to happen and not wanting it to happen all at the same time.

Getting more and more suspicious, I asked, "What's the matter with you?"

He looked surprised and said, "Nothing. Why?"

I went back to my language-arts assignment without answering him, so as not to give him any ideas about pestering me.

Lunchtime came. Still not a word. He didn't even look at me during lunch. I decided he must have forgotten all about tutoring.

When I finished eating, Patricia, Claudia, and I started to go to the schoolyard. We got as far as the double doors when T.J. shot in front of us and spread his arms across the doors.

"Wrong way," he said.

"Look, you don't want to tutor me, and I don't . . ."

"Oh, yes, I do. Come on," he said and pulled at me.

"Leave her alone, T.J." said Claudia.

"Get off me." I jerked away.

He looked me up and down, then walked off and over the lunchroom noise said, "It's your math grade, not mine."

"Right," I yelled back.

"What does he know, anyway?" Patricia asked. "Ignore him." She linked her arm through mine.

I tried to follow Patricia's advice, but as we were walking across the yard, I thought it over. "He's right," I said and drew away from her.

"You're going to let that creature teach you math?" Claudia asked.

"I guess."

"Are you crazy or what?" asked Patricia.

Maybe I was; maybe I wasn't. But despite T.J. and what my friends said, I had to go through with the tutoring.

"See you later," I told them and ran back inside. T.J. was halfway down the corridor when I caught up to him. I followed him to the second floor. The library was on the third.

"Where are you going?" I asked.

"You'll see."

At the end of the corridor was the auditorium. During lunch period, unless it was raining or snow-ing, it was empty. T.J. stopped in front of the projection room, which is up a short flight of stairs outside the rear of the auditorium.

"We're not supposed to be in here," I said.

"The kid who sets up the film for assembly is absent," T.J. said. "I'm taking his place."

"What about the library? The library teacher will get mad if we don't show up."

He waggled his hand and opened the door. A blast of air hit me in the face. The room was like a black pit. I followed him inside to look around. He shut the door behind us.

"Turn on the lights right now or I'll scream," I said, tripping over a step.

"And get everyone running here? They'll think we were kissing." He made kissing noises.

"T.J., I mean it."

"Okay. Okay." He flicked a switch, and the lights came on. "Besides, I'd never kiss you. I might turn into a frog." He thought he was so funny.

"No chance of that," I said, "since you're already a toad."

"We're wasting time," he said. He put his books on the table. I didn't budge. "Don't just stand there," he said, pulling out a chair.

Mr. Martinez came inside a moment later. "Is the film ready?"

T.J. cleared his throat. "I was going to tutor Barbra first."

"You were assigned to the library."

"Yes, but we took too long eating, and since I have to set up, I thought . . ."

Mr. Martinez checked his watch, then said, "You're right, stay here, and I'll inform the library teacher. I'll be next door if you need me."

When Mr. Martinez was gone, I said, "If you had permission to be here, why didn't you just tell me? Why were you being so sneaky?"

" 'Cause you're always so suspicious."

"For good reasons, too," I said, making a face, and reluctantly sat opposite him. Our knees touched and I drew back.

"Well?" he asked as if reading my thoughts.

"Well, yourself. You're supposed to tutor me. Tutor away!"

First he made me show him last night's homework. Although we were studying long division in class, there were also five word problems on the page. One look at my work and T.J. ran his fingers through his hair thoughtfully. Finally he said, "Let's start with division." He explained the first few problems.

"Understand?" he asked.

When I didn't answer, he explained another one. He ripped a sheet of paper from his spiral notebook and gave me a pencil. "Okay, do the rest by yourself," he said.

"I don't get it."

"Then let's do it step by step." He moved closer to me.

I moved away. "Not math," I said. "You. What are you up to? How come Mrs. Stone assigned *you* to me? And why are you acting nice?"

Instead of responding, he wiggled his eyebrows up and down.

"Hmmp!" I threw the pencil down.

"Get working," he said. He put the pencil back into my hand. "Remember—first try to estimate the quotient; multiply; subtract; and then bring down, the way I showed you."

I folded my arms. "Answer me. What's up your sleeve?"

He pushed up his sleeves. "Elbows."

"Ha! Ha!" I snatched up the paper and began working. T.J. whistled. From the inside pocket of his notebook, he took out squares of origami paper. While I worked on the page of problems, he folded the colored papers into airplanes. Although I kept glancing up at him, he was involved with his origami and never even looked at me.

I gave him the page of math problems to check. He made big red X's up and down the page, saying, "Wrong. Wrong. Wrong. You didn't listen to a word I said."

"Impossible." I felt prickly inside. It was almost as bad as when Mrs. Stone marks me wrong.

"Take my word for it. They're as wrong as wrong can be."

"You're not the teacher."

He shrugged and said, "Have it your way." Then he began to set up the film projector. I pushed him out of the way and left the room.

I didn't give math another thought until it was time to go over the homework later that afternoon. Of course, Mrs. Stone called me to the board. All eyes were on me as I put up the problem. When I was through, I sat down.

"Well, Barbra, how did you get that answer?" Mrs. Stone asked.

"Divided," I said, twisting my fingers around each other.

"You've given a new meaning to the process of division," she said, and the class snickered.

Sliding down in my seat, I wanted to disappear into the darkest corner of my desk.

T.J. stuck a note under my textbook. It said, "You should have listened to me."

"Jump in the lake," I wrote back.

He passed me another note that had a drawing—wavy lines for water and a stick figure getting ready to jump.

After school, I ran outside. Bright sunlight glinted off the mounds of snow piled up at the curb. A bunch of little kids were lying on their stomachs on the snow mounds, throwing snowballs at passing cars.

"Remember when we used to play mountain?"

I jumped at the sound of T.J.'s voice behind me. "Too bad I'm too big to play it now," I said.

"Who said? Come on."

"No way."

He made a snowball anyway, aimed it at a parked car, then spun around and tossed it at me. It hit me on the arm, but it was too soft to hurt.

"You rat!" I threw down my schoolbag, scooped up a handful of snow, and chased him. He ducked behind parked cars, trying to get out of my way. I sneaked up and splattered him. He had some snow in his hand and squashed it in my face, then took off down the street, laughing. The wind and bits of snow on my face felt so cool. I could have stayed there playing all afternoon. But Greg walked by and spoiled everything. He made jokes about me being T.J.'s girlfriend.

"Moron!" T.J. shouted, throwing a huge snowball at him. Greg ran down the street, laughing.

Me and T.J. That *was* a joke, but I was glad he stuck up for me. After that, we brushed the snow from our clothes, gathered up our schoolbooks, and started home.

"Ice-skating trip is Friday," he said when we reached my corner. "You going?"

Because I wasn't sure why he asked that, I said, "I don't know."

"Don't you like skating?" he asked, puzzled.

"Not really," I said and shrugged my shoulders.

"It's great! How can you *not* like it?"

I glared at him. "I just don't. Okay?" What I really wanted was for him to stop asking so many questions.

"If you can't skate, I'll teach you."

"Teaching me math is enough, don't you think?" I pushed him aside and went home.

Later that evening, the telephone rang. Billy answered it. "It's T.J."

"Talk to him, then," I went back to the book I was reading.

"He wants you," Billy said.

"Me?" Why was he calling me? He never called me before. I didn't want to talk to him.

Ma and Billy were both looking at me. So I dragged the telephone into the stuffy, dark hall closet, which smelled of mothballs and cardboard.

"What do you want, T.J.?"

"You need help with tonight's homework, don't you?"

"Did you call to tell me I'm an idiot, Anthony Jordan Brodie? That I can't figure out one little thing by myself?"

48

"No, I . . . Let's do the word problems this time."

He seemed serious. And I did need help. I brought my books into the closet, turned on the light, and sat down on a lumpy box.

He read," 'Nancy Jensen bought a TV for $638 and used it for twelve and one half years.' "

"That's ridiculous. Who cares how long she used it?"

"It's just a problem. Now, 'what was the cost of the TV per year?' *Per* means *each*. So, do you know what *per* tells you to do?"

"Any idiot knows that." I bit at a fingernail, thinking. "Six hundred fifty dollars and fifty cents?"

There was a pause, and then T.J. said, "You added. Why?"

"Should I have subtracted?"

"Why?"

"You're the tutor," I shouted. "You tell me."

"What's the key word?"

Boy, he sounded just like Mrs. Stone, answering a question with a question, never giving the answer.

"I guess it's not *TV*, huh? How about *cost*?"

"Don't you have that list we made in class?"

I turned back the pages of my notebook until I found the list of key words we had made in class months ago. I found *per* and *each* in the division group. T.J. told me to figure out what to do from the key words before solving any problem. Mrs.

49

Stone had said the same thing, but it hadn't made sense then. I tried it now, and it worked!

"My goodness, this isn't all that hard."

"You have to know what the problem is asking, though. Memorize the key words," he said. "Then doing word problems is a snap."

"All right," I said, knowing I could do that, since my memory was really good. If only I had memorized this list sooner.

"Back to Nancy Jensen," he said.

I groaned. "I hate division."

"Go on, you can do it," he urged.

"At least, it's not *long* division, but I can't divide twelve . . . That means I have to change twelve and one half into an improper fraction?" I said as I wrote the numbers on my paper. Why did textbooks have to be so tricky? Division, fractions, and word problems, too!

"Remember to invert," he said quickly.

"Always," I said. I scratched out the numbers and started all over, this time inverting the fraction. He must be some kind of mind reader. Finally, I got the answer, crossed my fingers, and said, "Fifty-one dollars and four cents?"

"Bingo!"

After doing the rest of the page, I asked, "You sure these are all right?"

"If you don't trust me, ask Billy."

"I will. Don't worry," I said, carefully slipping the page of completed problems into my notebook.

For what seemed like a long time, the only sound coming through the telephone was hissing static. It was as if we each wanted to say something but didn't know what.

Finally I said, "I have to go now."

"Me, too," he said and hung up.

Ice–Skating Party

———— o o ————

ON THE DAY of the ice-skating trip, the classroom was a din of noise. Every kid was chitter-chattering, even the quiet ones. Boys and girls were dressed in bright-colored sweaters or parkas with matching hats, wool scarves, and mittens. Mrs. Stone wore her regular clothes. Although it was her tradition to take her sixth-grade class ice-skating, she never skated.

I sat on Patricia's desk and picked up her brand-new skates. She had attached purple pom-poms to the laces. Claudia had new skates, too.

"They're figure skates," Patricia said with emphasis.

I ran my finger over the thin, shiny blade, feeling jealous of them. "Lucky! I didn't even think to ask my mother to buy me skates."

"The rental skates are just as good," said Claudia. But I knew better. Rental skates looked like boys' skates and were sometimes worn out.

To get our attention, Mrs. Stone had to ring the

bell on her desk. When we quieted down, she said, "Remember, Felicia's mother, Mrs. Williams, has given her time to us today. Let's all thank her now."

The class said "Thank you" in unison, and Mrs. Williams nodded. She was a small woman and looked nervous, sitting in the corner watching us.

"All right, people," Mrs. Stone said. "It's time to go."

Randy called out, "We gotta wait for T.J."

"Five minutes more," Mrs. Stone said, gathering up her hat and gloves.

More than five minutes went by, and still no T.J. The bus driver was beeping his horn for us. Claudia, Patricia, and I raced for the back row. We loaded the empty seat next to me with the dance bags, skates, hats, and gloves, so nobody else could sit with us. As I was arranging everything, I noticed T.J. running down the block, his knapsack and ice skates flopping against his shoulder. He waved for the bus to wait, but the bus driver was pulling away from the curb.

"Wait! T.J.'s here," I shouted.

"Yeah," said Greg. "Don't leave her boyfriend behind."

"Shut up, knucklehead," I said.

Patricia gave me a dirty look as T.J. hopped on the bus.

It took a long time to get to the rink, with all the traffic lights. Kids kept asking when were we going to get there. Mrs. Stone kept saying, "Soon." At last the bus reached the ice-skating rink, and everyone cheered. The driver parked behind a long line of other yellow school buses. Obviously, a lot of classes were on trips here today.

The dressing room, jammed with kids from other schools, smelled of wet rubber and sweaty socks. Since I had to wait in the skate-rental line, Claudia and Patricia were finished lacing their skates before me.

"We'll meet you outside," Claudia said and followed Patricia, leaving me in the dressing room alone.

When I finally exchanged my shoes for skates, I put them on and wobbled outside into the sunshine. Kids and a few grownups skated to the music blasting through the loudspeaker. Mrs. Stone and Felicia Williams's mother sat at a table, drinking coffee and eating Danish. Patricia and Claudia were on the other side of the rink, skating together. Kim skated by herself. Dressed in a pink-and-white parka, she reminded me of the Easter bunny.

I stumbled along, trying to reach my friends. I called to them, but the music drowned me out. Then my skates slid out from under me, and I fell right on my behind.

Looking around self-consciously, I tried to get up but only slid down again. That's when I spotted T.J. He was sucking in his cheeks to keep from laughing.

He skated around me and scraped to a stop. Bits of ice sprayed my face.

"I hate you, Anthony Jordan Brodie," I cried, groping for the railing. As I pulled myself up, my legs splayed. Before I landed on the ice again, T.J. grabbed my hand and helped me get my balance.

"These stupid skates!"

"The trick is getting the laces tight around the ankles."

"I need my own skates."

"It's not the skates," he said. "I'll show you."

"I don't need any lacing-up lessons, thank you very much."

"Then you'll wobble all day and maybe even hurt your ankles."

"They're hurting already."

He took a T-shaped metal hook from his pocket. "You need to use this. Come on." He circled me easily, then stepped lightly off the ice. I wobbled after him and sank down on a bench. He knelt in front of me and relaced each skate, pulling the laces really tight.

"I'm going to die from lack of circulation," I said.

"Only if your heart's in your ankles." He giggled. "Now stand up."

My legs felt like stiff boards ready to snap in two, but I could actually stand. "Where'd you learn this?"

He shrugged. "From a book."

"And did you learn to skate from a book, too?"

"Yeah." He put on his gloves, "Want to skate?" he asked shyly.

For once, I skated on the blades and not on my ankles. It was a wonderful feeling. The slow skating music changed to Michael Jackson's "Thriller" and everyone began moving fast to the beat. Some junior-high-school kids danced on the ice. One boy did break dancing, spinning around on his backside, but the skating guards made him stop.

"I'm hungry," T.J. said. "Are you?"

"Uh-huh, I was going to eat . . ."

". . . with Claudia and Patricia," he said knowingly.

But they were nowhere in sight. I decided to go inside with T.J. and we got on the food line. When we reached the front, T.J. put five dollars down on the counter and ordered two pizzas and two hot cocoas.

"I have money," I said.

"My treat."

"But . . ."

The man handed T.J. the tray and said, "Next."

Walking outside, I tried to pay him back for my food, but he refused to take the money. He put the tray down on an empty table.

"You hit the lottery or something?" I asked, sitting down next to him, but he didn't answer.

The pizza was hot and gooey. T.J. pulled at the cheese on his slice, thinking hard about something.

"*Revenge of the Swamp Creatures* is playing," he said suddenly. "Want to go this afternoon?"

I nearly choked. "Are you nuts? Anyway, scary movies give me nightmares."

"How about the library? We can study our math."

"Give me a break. Huh?" I was beginning to feel uncomfortable. What was with him?

I stuffed the last of the pizza into my mouth. "Thanks for paying," I said and got up to find my friends. They were on the other side of the rink, sitting on a bench.

"What's so funny?" I asked when I saw them giggling.

Patricia waggled her hand. "You had to hear the whole thing."

"We looked everywhere for you," Claudia said, sliding over to make room for me. "Where were you?"

"Skating." I was lucky they hadn't seen me with T.J.

Patricia said apologetically, "We ate already."

"That's okay," Instead of telling them I'd eaten too, I said, "I'm not hungry."

Later, when we skated around, we nearly collided into T.J., Randy, and Greg. We all made faces at each other and skated off. I didn't see much of T.J. after that.

On the bus, everyone talked about what a great trip it had been. Even Mrs. Stone was smiling.

I sat quietly, thinking. It was a great trip except for the part about T.J. asking me to go to the movies. It was like being asked to go on a date!

"What's wrong, Barbra?" Claudia asked.

"Nothing."

"Didn't you have fun?" she asked.

"It was probably those dumb skates," said Patricia. "Make your mother get you the kind like ours."

"Yeah," I said, even though the skates worked out fine. What was happening between T.J. and me was confusing, but I didn't want to talk to Claudia and Patricia about it. I was glad they had to hurry off to their ballet class. I watched them walk down the block, their identical skates and dance bags swinging from their shoulders.

A block from school, T.J. caught up with me. He pulled down his cap and said, "I know a bookstore where you can read all you want. Nobody bothers you."

I shook my head no.

"It's still real early," he said. "I just thought you'd want to read the new Nina Bawden book."

"A new one?" Nina Bawden was my favorite author. The kids in her books have all kinds of exciting adventures, the kind I wished I had. They discover secret passages in old houses, escape from kidnappers and thieves, and one girl keeps a pet pig until her mother has it butchered and serves it for dinner.

"How did you know she's my favorite?" I asked.

He tapped his finger against his forehead and grinned. "Does your mother let you go downtown?" he asked, like he was so much older than me.

"Last summer Claudia and I went all the way to the Museum of Natural History together." I remembered it clearly because that was the day Patricia moved into Claudia's building. We met her when we got home from the museum.

"Just Claudia and you? By yourselves?" T.J interrupted my thoughts.

"That's right. We took the number 7 bus."

"Then, come on." He pulled at me, but I pulled away.

After all, I never went anyplace with him before. Not just him and me. But the weird thing was, I kind of wanted to.

"I knew it. You can't go," he said.

"Wrong." I tossed my head and strolled off ahead of him.

The bus was at the bus stop when we got there. It went down Fifth Avenue along Central Park. We got off at Fifty-second Street in front of B. Dalton Booksellers. Inside, a man sat at the door next to a

59

divided arch that reminded me of the airport when they check you over before letting you on the plane. We went through one side of the arch.

From ceiling to floor, the shelves were filled with books. There was a wonderful smell of ink and paper everywhere. We went down the escalator. More books!

In back was the children's section. Tables were piled high with tons of books of all shapes, colors, and sizes: picture books, fairy tales, animal stories, and Bible stories. Book posters hung on the wall. Mobiles suspended from the ceiling turned slowly.

I made a beeline for the *B*'s, but all I saw were paperback editions of the Nina Bawden books I had already read. "It's not here."

"If it's new, it's probably in the hardcover section," T.J. said and showed me where to look. He really knew his way around this place.

The Finding was the title. T.J. pulled it off the shelf. Even the opening sentences sounded mysterious: *No one knew where Alex came from. Only where he was Found.*

I sat down on the carpeted floor and started to read while T.J. browsed. He pulled out two paperbacks and a hardcover, then sat next to me.

I was so caught up in the book I paid attention to nothing going on around me. In a way, it was a sad story. Alex didn't have birthday parties. He had finding-day parties because his family celebrated the day they found him lying in the arms of a statue.

In the middle of chapter 2, I happened to glance up and saw a wiry-haired saleslady watching us while pretending to be straightening books on a table. It was probably against the law to read so much of a book with no intention of buying it. Although I didn't want to, I closed the book and said, "I think we'd better go now."

T.J. nodded but kept on reading. I shook him. "Boy, this is a good one!" He tapped the slick blue cover. It was by Virginia Hamilton and he said it was about the Halloween back in 1938 when the radio broadcast that Martians had landed on earth.

"That never happened," I said. "It was a story."

"I know, it was by a man named H. G. Wells."

I expected him to put the book back on the shelf, since it was an expensive hardcover. Instead, T.J. said he was going to take not only his books but mine, too.

"It costs $10.25. That's so much money," I said.

"Don't worry." He laid the book on his stack. How could he pay for them? No way he had that much money.

As we went up the escalator, I saw the saleslady picking up a telephone. Our eyes met in the glass. I shuddered.

Upstairs, T.J. said, "I changed my mind. I'm going to put some of these back."

"Just put everything back, okay? I don't really want a book anyway."

He looked puzzled as he stepped on the down escalator. I waited for him. He came back carrying the two hardcover books but no paperbacks. What's more, it seemed like his knapsack was bulging more than before. My knees felt weak. I was panicky and grabbed his sleeve.

"What's wrong?" he asked.

I didn't know how to ask about the books without sounding as if I was accusing him of stealing. I ended up stammering, "N-nothing."

He gave me a queer look, then walked ahead of me to the cash register. He fished out three $10 bills and paid for the books, then boldly marched through the store. When he went through the archway, I squeezed my eyes shut, expecting alarms and sirens to go off. All I heard was silence. I tore out of the store after him.

"What did you do with those other books?" I asked while we waited on the corner for the light to turn green.

"Put them back. What do you think?"

"Well, I, uh . . ."

His eyes got wide. "You thought I stole them?"

"Don't be silly," I said and tried to laugh it off.

"I don't steal. Here. Check for yourself." He pushed his knapsack at me.

"Forget it," I said.

He pulled the zipper with a yank and shook the contents on the ground. Passersby glanced at us, but no one stopped to look at the assortment of things tumbling from his knapsack—a packet of Oreo cookies, an orange, origami papers, some letters bound together with a rubber band, the tape cassettes, and library books. I had no business thinking such bad things about him, and I apologized. But T.J. refused to talk to me.

I tried to make him laugh by telling a joke. "A woman said to her husband, 'Oh, dear, I think I hear a mouse squeaking.' What do you think the husband said? He said, 'So, what do you want me to do—oil it?' "

I giggled.

T.J. sulked.

"Get it—oil, squeaking . . . How about this one? 'Mommy, Mommy, I don't want to go to Australia.' 'Shut up and keep swimming.' "

"That's corny."

"You talked!" After a moment, I said, "I'm really sorry. That saleslady made me nervous. I never saw you with that much money before."

"Next, you'll ask where I stole the money from."

"Don't say that."

63

"For your information, my mother sent it to me. Her boss gave her a raise."

"That's great. When is she going to send for you?"

"Any day now. That's what she said in her letter. And I believe her, no matter what Pop says."

Suddenly I was missing him already. But that was crazy. This was T.J., the pest, the pain in the neck. Today, though, he felt like a friend.

On the bus ride uptown, we sat side by side, talking now and then about what we were reading.

"It must be awful to know you're unwanted," T.J. said as he handed my book back to me.

"In a way, I don't want Alex's real mother to come back. He's been living with his adopted family all his life. He belongs with them."

"It's a story," T.J. said. "So his mother probably doesn't come back."

"Do you mean . . . ?" I stopped myself. It seemed as if T.J. was saying that mothers in real life didn't abandon their children. Hadn't he ever watched news reports about mothers who put babies in shopping bags and left them on doorsteps or in trash cans? How could he be so sure his mother was going to send for him after all this time? And the way he talked, it sounded as if he thought he was going away any day now.

64

Missing

—— ∘ ∘ ——

MONDAY MORNING, Mrs. Stone called me to her
desk. "Since Anthony isn't here to tutor you," she
said, "I'm giving you these problems to do."

I took the sheet of paper to my seat. When I sat
down, Kim tapped my shoulder. "Where's T.J.?"

"I don't know," I said. His desk with papers spill-
ing out and his empty seat looked so abandoned.

It had been two days since I last saw T.J. He and
his grandfather missed church, which was odd, because even when Mr. Treadwell is sick, T.J. comes
to church by himself. I wondered whether his mother
sent for him or whether he was just home sick with
the flu.

At the end of the day, while everyone was copying
homework assignments and getting ready to go home,
I went to Mrs. Stone's desk and spoke quietly to
her.

"I'll take T.J.'s homework to him."

She nodded. "Good idea." She then gave me my math homework paper. There were more checks than X's.

"Keep up the good work," she said and smiled at me for the first time I could remember. I felt so proud of myself. A page of word problems, and only two mistakes! I could hardly wait to show T.J.

After school, I went straight to T.J.'s apartment. The first time I rang the bell, no one answered. I rang two more times and then heard locks being turned. Mr. Treadwell opened the door dressed in a checked robe and slippers. He leaned heavily on his cane.

"What do you want?" he asked.

I shifted the books in my arms. "Uh, I came to give T.J. his homework."

"He's not here."

I peeked through the crack in the door. I could see almost the whole living room and part of the kitchen. Over the back of a chair hung T.J.'s knapsack, but before I could ask about the knapsack, Mr. Treadwell closed the door.

The next day, when I told Mrs. Stone about not being able to give T.J. his homework, she said, "I'm sure there's nothing to worry about." And I believed her until Friday when weird things started to happen.

First, Mrs. Stone took attendance as usual, but

when she got to T.J.'s name, she skipped right over him.

"Mrs. Stone, you didn't call T.J.," Randy called out.

She looked over the rim of her glasses and said, "I know."

"Is he sick or something?" Jorge asked.

"He's fine," Mrs. Stone said, "but I'm not allowed to discuss the details."

What details, I wondered. I waited until lunch-time to talk to Randy. He might know something. I eased my way through the line to where he was. "When was the last time you saw T.J.?" I asked.

"After supper, Friday, I think," he said, picking up his tray.

"Me, too. What about Saturday or Sunday?"

He handed the lunch lady his tray and told her, "Extra corn." Turning to me, he said, "Why are you so interested?"

I grunted. "He's supposed to be tutoring me," I said and walked off. But I couldn't help wondering why Mrs. Stone skipped over T.J.'s name.

The other weird thing happened at the end of the day. Mrs. Stone told me she was going to look for another tutor for me.

"Why?" I asked. "T.J. was . . . is the best math student in the class. You said so yourself."

"Barbra," she said, sounding annoyed. "Your

grades are getting better. Don't you want to keep improving?"

"Yes, but . . ."

"Good." She pushed back her chair and stood up as if everything was settled.

"I'll wait for T.J. He'll be back soon. Won't he?"

"I certainly hope so," she said. "However only three months of school are left. Why ruin it?"

"I just don't understand."

She patted my hand. "There's nothing to worry about." That was the second time she'd said those words about T.J. This time, instead of comforting me, her kind words made me shudder. "Now run along."

While she put a stack of papers into her briefcase, I stood there watching her. She snapped her briefcase shut. "Barbra, standing here is not going to solve anything."

"Can't you tell me where he is?"

She shook her head. "I'm sorry. It's against school policy to discuss one student with another." She turned off the classroom light. "I'm sure you're eager to get your weekend started. Any plans?"

"No," I said, although Claudia, Patricia, and I planned on going bicycle riding.

Thick dark clouds hung low in the sky Saturday morning. Because it was raining, Claudia and I spent the afternoon at Patricia's house. It was Patricia's idea to make pizza. She had all the ingredients and her mother wasn't fussy about the kitchen.

Making the pizza was fun. We each took turns throwing the circle of dough into the air, the way they do at the pizzeria. When the dough turned gray, we decided it was time to use it. Patricia smoothed it into a pan. Claudia poured on the sauce. I sprinkled on the grated cheese.

While the pizza cooked, we sat on the floor in Patricia's room. The furniture and walls were white. The curtains and carpeting were red. Her ruffled bedspread was white, sprinkled with tiny red roses. It was too showy. I liked the plainness of my beige walls, dark-green bedspread, and maple furniture.

We danced to a Lisa Lisa album until we got tired. We flopped down on the bed and ogled guys in rock magazines and practiced kissing by pressing our lips against the glossy, cold pages.

Claudia ran her tongue over her braces and said, "I wonder what the real thing is like."

Patricia's knowing answer was, "Warm and wonderful."

The oven timer rang, signaling that the pizza was ready. We ate until we were stuffed. Then Patricia hustled us back into her room as if we were on a secret mission.

Shutting the door, she said, "Let's call somebody."

"Somebody like who?" I asked.

"Anybody."

"You mean like strangers? Billy and I used to do that when we were little. Once we called a lady and said her slip was showing. When the telephone bill came, my mother had a fit. We had called Arizona. And she made us pay for the call. It cost only a dollar and some change, but it seemed like a lot then."

Patricia flicked her wrist. "We're not calling strangers," she said. "We're going to call up boys." At that, Claudia covered her mouth and giggled.

It seemed like a babyish thing to do, especially since Patricia disguised her voice by talking into a glass.

"Your turn." Patricia passed the glass to me after Claudia made her call. "Who do you want to call?"

"No one." I put the glass down on her night table.

"You're no fun," said Patricia.

"I just don't feel like it," I said.

"Sometimes you act like such a goody-goody."

"I do not. I don't have to do everything you want to do."

She rolled her tongue in her cheek. "Maybe it's because she doesn't know any boys," she said to Claudia.

"I don't want to play. Okay?" It was bad enough that it was a silly game. Trying to force me to play was worse.

Patricia pulled out the thick telephone book and flipped through the pages. "Ah-ha!" She punched out a telephone number.

"Who are you calling?" I asked.

"Hell-o," she said into the telephone. "Is T.J. home? . . . Yes, I'll hold."

I could not believe she had actually called T.J. and that he was home. I snatched the telephone from her. "T.J., where in the world have you been?" I blurted before I realized I was talking to a recording of the weather.

Patricia laughed. "She fell for it." She nudged Claudia, and she began laughing, too.

"That's not funny." I slammed the phone down so hard that both girls jumped.

"Maybe it wasn't a good idea," said Claudia, cautiously.

Patricia sucked her teeth in disgust. "Where's your sense of humor? You both act like real nerds. Jeez, making a federal case from a little joke. Besides, he's not home, anyway."

"How do you know?" I asked.

She flexed and pointed her toes, then did some ballet steps around the chair. "Mr. Treadwell goes to my father's barber shop. I heard T.J.'s grandfather tell my father how much trouble T.J. is." She stopped and looked me straight in the face. "He's locked up in one of those places for bad kids."

71

"He is not."

Patricia elbowed Claudia. "I told you she'd say that." And Claudia said, "Uh-huh."

It was the two of them against me. I didn't feel like staying there any longer and went home.

The apartment was silent except for the hum of the refrigerator. I tried to read the book T.J. had bought me but kept thinking about him and what Patricia had said. I knew she was wrong, but I still wanted to know why he hadn't been in school and why Mrs. Stone had skipped his name. Maybe his mother had sent for him, but then why did he leave his knapsack behind? I had so many questions. Nobody wanted to tell me anything—not Mrs. Stone, not Mr. Treadwell.

The next day, Mr. Treadwell was back in church, without T.J. I turned around to speak to him, but he looked past me and didn't say a word. Instead of listening to the rest of the service, I was trying to think of a way to get Mr. Treadwell to talk to me. At the very end of the service, when Ma and the rest of the choir filed up the aisle, I followed them into their dressing room. The women were talking as they took off their shiny choir robes. Ma was in the corner, hanging up her robe.

"Ma, you have to talk to Mr. Treadwell about T.J."

Smoothing out her dress, she asked, "What about?"

"T.J.'s missing!"

"Oh, Barbra," she said tiredly.

72

"All week!"

Ma touched my face, smiling as if I'd said something ridiculous.

I pulled away from her. "It's true."

"Mr. Treadwell hasn't said a word about it."

"That's the whole point." I strained to whisper to keep the other women from hearing. "Mr. Treadwell must know where he is, but he won't say anything."

Ma thought a moment, then said hurriedly, "We have to get home."

"Please, Ma. You wanted T.J. and me to get along. We were starting to, and now he's gone. Can't you just ask Mr. Treadwell where he is?"

Finally she agreed, and we went outside to meet Billy and try to find Mr. Treadwell before he went home.

At the top of the stairs, I searched over everyone's head. Billy spotted Mr. Treadwell walking down the block. When we caught up to him, Ma spoke politely and asked how he was feeling.

"Don't fret about me," he said.

She talked about the weather, the sermon, everything except T.J. I nudged her. She finally said, "We've missed T.J."

I held my breath. He would have to tell her. She was another grownup.

His breathing was loud and raspy. "He's with relations down South."

"Can I call him?" I asked.

"They don't have a phone," he said, nodded to Ma, and limped away.

"That doesn't make sense," I said.

"It makes perfect sense," said Ma. "Raising children isn't easy. Mr. Treadwell is not a young man and he isn't well. Relatives can probably care for T.J. better until Irene sends for him."

"Something happened to him."

"Ma's right," said Billy. "Stop exaggerating."

Billy and I lagged behind Ma. "I have proof," I said in a low voice.

"Yeah, what?"

"His knapsack. I saw it. T.J. would never go away and leave it."

"Unless he didn't want it anymore, or he got a new one," Billy said reasonably.

I went on. "But suppose he really is at home, why doesn't he come to school?"

"Maybe his mother sent for him, after all."

"Then why didn't Mr. Treadwell just say so?"

"Well, only two people know for sure what happened—Mr. Treadwell and T.J. himself."

My brainy brother was wrong. Three people knew the truth about T.J.'s disappearance. Mr. Treadwell, T.J., *and* Mrs. Stone. And I was going to be the fourth.

Mystery Friend

———— o o ————

IT WAS easy enough to get back inside the school building Monday after school. The trouble was getting into the classroom—the door was locked. My only hope was that Miss Cora, the cleaning lady, would let me inside. Her cleaning wagon was parked in front of the room next door to my classroom.

She came out to empty a wastepaper basket. "School's dismissed," she said. "Go home."

"Can you open my classroom?" I asked. "I forgot a book."

"It'll be there tomorrow." She went back inside, pushing her wide bristle broom over the floor.

"I need my math book," I said, following her. "We're having a big test."

She shot a suspicious glance at me. I was so close to her I could see the stiff hairs growing out of her chin.

"I might fail math." The truth of those words

and the lie they covered up gave me a sharp ache inside.

She propped her broom against the wall, then shuffled to my classroom. "You kids! Good thing your heads are screwed on. You'd forget them, too." She unlocked the door and pushed it open. "Don't take all day."

I stood stock-still until I heard her broom bumping against the metal legs of the kids' desks next door. Then I tiptoed up to Mrs. Stone's desk and opened the middle drawer. Being careful not to disturb anything, I took out the red roll book and flipped over each attendance card, one by one. Angie Young's card was the last. Behind hers was an orange sheet of paper and behind that was what I was looking for—T.J.'s card. At the bottom, next to the words *Discharged to*, was written P.S. 187X.

I had no idea where that school was. As I was about to close the roll book, I noticed two sets of envelopes stapled to the inside of the roll-book cover. They held slips for Admissions and Discharges. T.J.'s was the first slip on the discharge pile. His mother had not sent for him, and he was definitely not with relatives. He was in a place called Redding Group Home for Boys. So Patricia was right and Mr. Treadwell had lied to Ma!

When I heard footsteps in the hall, I quickly wrote down the address from the discharge slip, then stuffed the blue slips back into the envelope and put the roll book into the drawer.

When I started to leave, nosy Kim was standing in the doorway, holding her schoolbooks.

"Barbra? What are you doing here?" she asked, eyes wide.

"I . . . needed a pencil," I said and reached into Mrs. Stone's pencil can. It tumbled over. Pencils and pens spilled out and rolled onto the floor. If that wasn't bad enough, before I could put everything in order, Miss Cora came back.

Kim rushed to her seat, snatched up her sweater, and held it up for Miss Cora to see. "I came for this. See?"

"I can explain," I said, getting to my feet, putting the last of the pencils into the can, and slipping the piece of paper into my pocket.

"Explain it to your teacher." Miss Cora pointed to the door. "Out!"

On our way downstairs, I said to Kim, "I wasn't doing anything wrong." I pushed through the door and a blast of cold air hit my face. I hiked up my jacket collar.

"Tell me. It'll be our secret. Promise," she said, following me down the block.

"I was getting a pen," I said through clenched teeth, and looking straight ahead. "That's all."

"Before, you said pencil."

Throwing up my arms, I said, "Pencil, pen, I needed something to write with. Okay?"

"Then why were you looking in the roll book?"

I was too shocked to answer. All I could think of was, I'd been caught by Gumdrop, and that made me angry. "You snoop!" I shouted. "Sneaking up on a person like a thief."

"That's not true."

"Oh, no?"

Although I was as much a snoop as she, I had to make her feel guilty to keep her from tattling to Mrs. Stone. But no matter what I said, she would not go away. She tagged after me, matching her steps to mine. I walked fast; she walked fast. I crossed the street; so did she. By the time I reached my block, I was really fed up with her.

"Stop following me!"

Her bottom lip quivered. "I'm not. I live right over there." She pointed to a red-brick building with fire escapes on the front windows. I passed that building every day on my way to school, but I didn't know she lived there.

"Look, I have to go home and write my black-history report," I lied. The report was the last thing on my mind.

"Me, too. What are you doing?" she asked eagerly.

"The Montgomery boycotts."

"I'm doing Martin Luther King. We match." She smiled. "Let's work together."

I wanted to say "Get lost," but I said, "Okay," instead.

I thought that if I wasn't nice to her she'd go straight to Mrs. Stone first thing in the morning. It would be like the time she gave Mrs. Stone the letter from Ma. I took her home with me.

"You have an upstairs!" she said when she walked into the apartment and saw the staircase that led to our bedrooms. Most people, I guess, don't expect to see staircases inside an apartment.

"It's called a duplex." I put my books down on the Parsons table and hung up my coat. I draped hers over the table, hoping she'd get the message and go home soon.

Kim rubbed the shiny banister and dug her feet into the carpeting, like she was in the Taj Mahal. "May I look around?"

"It's just an apartment," I said.

"Please?"

I took her on a quick tour, pointing out each room. When we got to my mother's room, Kim took a step backwards.

"It's not holy ground. You can go inside."

"I feel funny going into your mother and father's room."

"My father died a long time ago." I told her how he died in the plane crash.

"Oh. I didn't know."

"That's my father." I pointed out the picture of

him in his Navy uniform. Along with the other family pictures, it hung on the wall opposite the stairs. I straightened it. "He was a hero."

"You look like him," she said.

"Everyone tells me I'm his spitting image." If only I had inherited his brains, too. Then getting rid of Kim would be a cinch.

"I love your house."

She'll be here forever, I thought, as I walked into the kitchen.

"These are the books I'm using for my report," she said, putting her stack of books down on the table. "There's a chapter on the Montgomery boycotts in this one, and lots of photographs, too."

I flipped through the glossy pages of the book. Kim made herself really comfortable and spread her notebook and supplies on the table.

"Don't you eat snacks after school?" she asked, eyeing the bowl of fruit in the center of the table.

"I'm dieting." That shut her up.

When Billy came downstairs to get a glass of milk and an apple, he didn't act surprised to see Kim. He even asked her about her brother. His name is Lamont and he was in the fifth grade.

"Lamont's on the baseball team," Billy said to me.

I frowned. "Are we talking or working?"

Kim lowered her head and leafed through the pages of her book. Billy poked me in the shoulder, then left the kitchen.

When I was in the middle of writing a list of the causes and effects of the Montgomery boycott, the telephone rang. It was Patricia.

"Why aren't you at ballet?" I asked.

"Canceled. A water pipe busted or something," she said breathlessly. "We're coming up to your apartment right now."

Why did Kim have to be here to ruin everything?

"No. Wait. I have company." I clamped my hand over my mouth. What a dumb thing to say!

"Company? Who?" Patricia asked.

"Uh, you don't know her."

"What's her name?"

"Her name? Uh, Bonny. She's not from around here," I added quickly. "She goes to a different school and everything."

"Where?"

"Um . . ."

"Never mind," Patricia said, impatiently. "I'll ask her myself."

Trying to stall her, I said, "How about buying us some sodas? Maybe some Doritos, too?"

"Soda makes me break out. Besides, I want to meet Bonny. God, where did she get that name? We're on our way," she said and hung up.

I felt bad for lying, for denying Kim was here, yet they were my friends, not her. I stared into the refrigerator at covered bowls of leftover food while

81

I tried to figure out a way of getting rid of Kim without hurting her feelings.

"Aren't you tired of homework?" I asked, slamming the door shut. "I am. Besides, I really shouldn't have company after four o'clock."

"That's why Patricia and Claudia are coming over?" She started gathering up her stuff.

"Wait." I wanted to say something nice, but the doorbell rang before I could think of anything. What was I going to do? If Patricia found Kim here, she would flip.

Patricia banged on the door, shouting, "Open up!"

Kim stood in the doorway with frightened eyes. When I said, "It's them," she ducked back into the kitchen.

"Not there," I said. The kitchen was a lousy place to hide. But where else could she go? Patricia was banging and Billy was yelling at me to open the door. I took a long breath, wiped my clammy hands on my skirt, and let them in.

"Where's this Bonny, the mystery friend?" Patricia asked, barging into the living room.

"You got here so fast," I said.

"We were in the lobby."

"Patricia bet me it was a boy," said Claudia, looking around expectantly.

I scratched my arm. "You crazy? There's no boy here, unless you count Billy."

Patricia peeked under the sofa, the chairs, even under the lamp tables, while Claudia tagged after her, saying, "Come out, come out, wherever you are."

A clumping noise came from over our heads. Kim was upstairs! Patricia ran up the stairs. She was about to open Billy's door when he shouted, "Open this door and you're dead meat."

"It's me—Patricia," she said.

"No girls allowed."

She went into my room and pushed open the door.

"You're wasting your time," I said, crossing my fingers. "She left already."

Patricia brushed past me and burst into Ma's room as if it were her own. Claudia was right behind her. It was strange to see Claudia act like this. She never tromped all over my house before.

"You can't go into my mother's room," I said, thinking Kim might be hiding in there. "You have to come out."

Patricia skipped down the stairs. "There's only one place left."

"The kitchen," Claudia said.

They inspected the kitchen, throwing open every cupboard door, as if someone could be hiding behind the cups and saucers. How stupid could they be!

Kim was gone. Somehow she got out without being seen. Thank goodness!

83

"You were telling the truth," Patricia said, surprised. "The mystery friend is really gone."

"I told you."

"I never heard of a Bonny before," Claudia said.

"She's a cousin, second cousin." I felt hot and sweaty.

"Your cousins live in Philadelphia," said Claudia.

"All . . . except this one. She just moved to Brooklyn. You must've seen her on your way up."

"We didn't see anybody," said Patricia suspiciously.

I licked my lips, thinking. "How about a snack?" I asked quickly, and put on the table boxes of Oreos and graham crackers and a container of milk and a jar of peanut butter, since I knew Claudia loved eating graham crackers spread with peanut butter.

Pushing the jar away, Claudia said, "Sticks to my braces," and drank a glass of milk instead.

Patricia took a ripe pear from the fruit bowl and chomped on it as she talked about starting a club.

"I've always wanted to be in a club," I said. "We started one in third grade. Remember, Claudia?"

"It was a flop, though."

"This is going to be the best club ever," said Patricia, picking up the green-and-silver pen that was on the table.

I shuddered when Patricia turned it over. I was afraid she'd realize it was Kim's, but she merely said, "Got another pen that's not so yucky?"

I gave her mine, and when she wasn't looking, I slid Kim's pen out of sight behind the napkin holder.

She tore a sheet of paper from my notebook. "We're going to buy T-shirts and have our club name printed on them and everything. We need officers."

"I think Patricia should be president, since she thought of the club first," Claudia said.

"Thanks," Patricia said and wrote her name under the word *President*.

It seemed like they had already planned everything and I was just finding out about it now. It was as if they were best friends and I was an outsider.

"Barbra?" Patricia shook my arm.

"Huh?"

"I said, is it okay with you—I mean, that I be president?"

I suppose she wondered why I hadn't agreed with Claudia. So I said, "Shouldn't we vote? It's not really fair unless we vote."

Patricia wrinkled up her nose. "Why—won't you vote for me?"

I looked at Claudia to say something. She flicked her wrist, copying Patricia's habit, and said, "It's a waste of time. There're only three of us. And Patricia will make a great president."

"I second that," Patricia said. She and Claudia giggled.

I finally gave in. After all, it really was the two of them against me.

Under her name, Patricia wrote *Vice president*. Claudia raised her hand and said, "Me."

"All opposed?" Patricia asked. Of course, no hands went up. "It's settled," she said.

Then she turned to me. "Which job do you want?"

They just did not understand about fairness, and it was useless to try to explain. "Treasurer," I said.

Patricia eyed me warily. "Why not secretary? Your handwriting is way better than your math."

It hurt that she was using my being a lousy math student against me. "I'm getting better," I wanted to say, but I didn't think it would make a difference.

"Be secretary," Patricia said. "You have the best handwriting. We need that for minutes and stuff."

I agreed.

She went on to say, "You have to buy a notebook. Red. We're calling ourselves the Red-Hot Ladies."

"What are we going to do?" I asked.

"I already told you. We're going to wear red shirts with our names printed on them."

"We'll have meetings and do everything together," added Claudia.

"But mostly," Patricia said, "it's being in the club that matters and that only club members are invited to my slumber party."

"That means us," Claudia said proudly.

Although I was glad I was part of the club, I wished they hadn't figured out everything without me. After they left, I started cleaning off the table, then remembered about T.J. and went straight to Billy's room. I was halfway up the stairs when his door opened.

He peeped out. "Are they gone yet?"

"Uh-huh." Before I could tell Billy the news about T.J., Kim crept from behind him. Her coat, sweater, and books were bundled up in her arms. She had been hiding in Billy's room all along.

"I'm going home now," she said.

"They won't be back," I said lamely and felt like kicking myself.

"They might, and they'd only make fun of me." She walked down the stairs and out of the apartment. I wanted to call her back but couldn't.

Billy looked at me disgustedly. "Why do you treat her that way?"

"It's not my fault," I said.

"Never is." He went into his room and began tinkering with his trains. "You shouldn't have invited her here if you . . ."

"Me? Invite her?" I wanted to tell him about all the trouble Kim caused me, but that wasn't important now. "I know where he is."

"Where *who* is?"

"Who's the only person missing around here?"

He turned off the electric trains. "How did you find out?"

"Never mind. He's in a place called Redding Group Home." I took the paper from my pocket and showed it to him.

Neither one of us knew what kind of place Redding Group Home was. I did know that kids were sent to homes and shelters if they were juvenile delinquents or orphans. T.J. was neither. The reason he was in a home was a mystery. But not how he got there. That was plain enough.

"Mr. Treadwell put T.J. there," I said. "No wonder he's keeping it a secret! It's so nobody'll know what he did."

"His own grandfather put him in a home?" Billy asked. "You sure?"

"Who else?" Then I remembered something. "Patricia even overheard Mr. Treadwell talking about it. I bet he took T.J. to that place Friday evening after he came home from the bookstore."

"Why?" Billy looked skeptical. "His own grandfather?"

As unbelievable as it seemed, it was the only thing that fit, and one telephone call to T.J. would prove it. After getting the telephone number from information, I called Redding Group Home.

A woman with a Southern accent answered. "T.J. can't come to the telephone," she said. "He's with his case worker."

"Can he call me back?"

"That's up to his case worker. Give me your number, I'll get back to you."

I waited and waited for her call. After forty minutes went by, I called the home again. The woman told me that T.J.'s case worker had left already.

"But I have to talk to T.J. now. It's important," I said.

"You can't," she said.

"Why not?"

"I don't have time to explain the procedures," she said, sounding like a recording. "I told you the first time you called that I'd have to talk to his case worker, and I will just as soon as I can."

"Never mind," I said. "When do people visit?"

"From four till seven o'clock. Why?"

"No reason. Bye," I said quickly and hung up before she could tell me not to come. I had made up my mind. I was going to see T.J. and nothing was going to stop me. Putting away the telephone book, I smiled to myself, thinking how surprised T.J. would be to see me.

P.S. Write Back!

———— o o ————

"LATE," Mrs. Stone said when I walked into the room the next day. Mrs. Stone stood in front of the classroom, holding the opened roll book.

Right away I knew something was wrong. No one was laughing, talking, or sharpening pencils. I stood frozen at the door. Everyone was looking at me. Obviously, they all knew that I had been in the room after school yesterday and had gone through the roll book. Miss Cora must have told Mrs. Stone. Or was it Kim? Kim turned away, refusing to look at me.

"Whenever you're ready, Barbra," Mrs. Stone said, her head bobbing slightly.

My voice cracked when I said, "May I speak with you later, Mrs. Stone, to explain? I had a good reason."

"Do you have a note?"

"Note? Uh-uh, I don't have one."

"Then there's no excuse." She faced the entire class. "That goes for the rest of the latecomers." She called them by name. "Kim, Carlos, Greg, Felicia, and now you, Barbra. Don't think that because you're sixth-graders you can do as you please." She looked at me again as if studying me. I shifted from one foot to the other. "Sit down, Barbra. We've wasted enough time."

After I slid into my seat, she snapped the roll book shut and said, "Lateness will reflect on your report card. I suggest you start developing better habits. Junior-high-school teachers are less tolerant than I am."

Being late for school? That was the only reason she was angry? It seemed a little thing to be giving us such a big lecture about. But that meant she didn't know about me and the roll book—yet.

The whole day went by and not one word about the roll book. I finally decided it was dumb to worry about anyone finding out. If Kim was going to tattle, she would have done it already. I guess she wasn't as bad as everybody thought.

Billy was in the kitchen eating cookies and drinking a glass of chocolate milk when I got home. Somehow, he always managed to get home before me. I dumped my books beside his on the counter and poured myself some milk, too.

"Billy, old buddy? I need a loan. Two dollars."

He wiped milk from his mouth. "You never pay back."

"I will. I swear."

"What do I get?" he asked.

"I'll do your homework for a week."

He gave me a look. "No, thanks."

"Well, I'll pay interest like it's a real loan."

"It is a real loan," he said. From his wallet he took two crisp dollar bills. "What do you need it for, anyway?"

"Why do you have to know?" I pocketed the money before he changed his mind and then searched the kitchen drawers for a small paper bag.

"I think I already do, and you're crazy. Suppose Ma calls?"

"Tell her . . ."

"Don't think I'm going to lie for you."

"Who asked you to?" I slammed the drawer shut and filled the bag with an unopened packet of cookies, two granola bars, and a big navel orange.

As I was leaving the house, Billy called to me from the top of the stairs. He was silhouetted in the dim hall light. For a moment, I thought he was going to come along. All he said was, "Tell T.J. 'Hi' for me, and don't talk to any perverts."

It had turned cloudy outside. An icy chill was in the air as if it were going to snow. I buttoned my jacket up and hurried down the block toward the subway. When I was almost there, I heard a train rumble into the station. But getting tokens and directions made me miss it and I had to wait a long time for the next one.

It was a noisy, rocky ride to the Bronx. Finally my stop, Gun Hill Road, came. I got off and walked downstairs. There were all sorts of stores on the street. People picked over grapefruits and cabbages at the fruit-and-vegetable market. I asked the newsstand man how to find Redding Group Home. He didn't know until I showed him the address.

"Walk three blocks to Bronxwood," he said, pointing in the direction. "You'll pass Bojangles, the chicken place. Then turn right. You can't miss it."

He was right. Finding Bronxwood Avenue was easy. The block was lined with trees and private houses. A little girl in a blue snowsuit rode a tricycle up the block, making zooming noises. A fat gray cat lay curled up on a stoop, sleeping. Somehow, I didn't think Redding would be on this block, but the numbers were going in the right order.

3601 Bronxwood, unlike the private houses on the block, was a gray brick building. Although it looked ordinary on the outside, no telling what it was like on the inside. The main thing was that I was going to see T.J.

．　．　．

The room I entered was like a dentist's waiting room. There were old magazines on the table. Faded paintings of flowers in vases and of bowls of fruit hung on the wall. In a corner, a fake rubber tree leaned sideways, and one of its leaves lay on the floor. Though steam hissed through the radiator, the room was cold.

I followed the sound of a typewriter to an office. The light was so bright it was almost blinding. A woman with a long, blond braid was typing. On her desk was a candy jar filled with peppermints.

"May I help you?" she asked.

I squared my shoulders and said, "I'm here to see T.J. I mean Anthony Brodie."

She drew her eyebrows together. "You're the girl who called yesterday?"

"Yes."

"You're not allowed here."

"Why not?"

"Minors must be accompanied by an adult," she said in that recording voice.

"Why?"

"I don't make the rules, only follow them." Her telephone rang. She punched the lighted button and answered the phone.

When she hung up, I said, "I won't stay long. Promise. Just long enough to give him the stuff I brought."

"Sorry," she said.

"I came a long way." I didn't intend to come this far and not see T.J. Opposite this room was a stairway. I wondered if that led to where they were keeping him. I thought of sneaking up when her back was turned.

Her telephone rang again. She put her hand over the mouthpiece and said, "If you leave the bag, I'll give it to him."

I sat down, waiting for her to finish talking. I knew now that I wasn't going to see T.J., but I couldn't just leave, either. While I waited, I decided to write a letter to T.J. on the paper bag. It said:

Dear T.J.,

Surprise! Guess where I am writing this letter? Downstairs in the secretary's office. I tried to get in to see you, but they have a dumb rule about kids visiting. I don't have to ask why you're here. Your grandfather, right? I call that unfair. If I ever become a senator, I'll make laws against things like that. I never told anyone, but that's what I think I want to do—run for Congress. That way I can tell *other* people what to do for a change.

Here are your favorite cookies. Mine are real, not fake like yours. (Remember that wooden cookie?)

I finished reading *The Finding*. Now I'm going to reread *The Peppermint Pig* because I like the part when the butcher accidentally chops off Old Granny Greengrass's finger. I like another part too, but I won't tell you any more, in case you want to read the book.

Billy says, "Hi." And so do I.

Yours truly,
Barbra

P.S. Write back!

When the woman finished her phone call, she reached for the bag. "I'll see that he gets it."

"You sure I can't go see him? Maybe he can come down here."

"Rules are rules," she said. She unrolled the sheet of paper from her typewriter and rolled in another one. "You aren't even supposed to *be* here, which means I shouldn't be taking this bag, but I will. Then you have to go."

I handed her the bag so that the side with the letter written on it was out of sight.

She turned the bag over, anyway. "How sweet," she said after reading my letter. She put everything into a huge brown envelope and wrote T.J.'s name across the front and laid the envelope on a corner of her desk.

When I got home, Billy was watching the six-o'clock news. I told him what had happened.

"You think he'll write me back?"

"I don't know, Barbra," he said helplessly.

Not once during dinner did Billy say anything about my going up to Redding. I smiled at him. He smiled back.

Ma told us about seeing Mr. Treadwell in the grocery store. "He says T.J. is doing well. T.J. likes living with his aunt and uncle."

Billy and I looked at each other in astonishment. Ma went on, "I told Mr. Treadwell you might like to write to him. He promised T.J. would write to you soon. Does that make you feel better?"

It made me furious! But I couldn't say anything, not without telling Ma about the roll book and the trip to Redding Group Home. If she knew, she'd probably make me stay in my room forever. There would be no TV, no movies, no bike riding in the park, and no slumber parties, just one long punishment. For once, I chose my words very carefully and said, "That's good news. Isn't it, Billy?" He nodded.

After supper, I was getting ready to watch *Matlock*. Ma asked me about my math homework.

"I wanted to watch this show first."

"Homework's more important," she said and turned the TV off.

I stomped to my room and took out my books. I was trying to work out a word problem, but I kept thinking about T.J. being locked up and how Mr.

Treadwell had lied. Working out word problems was so dumb, compared to what was happening in real life. Why did math have to be so important? It was probably a stupid rule written down somewhere, I finally decided. Rules to do this; rules to do that. I was sick to death of rules. I flung the book aside.

One day I was going to change those dumb rules. Kids would be able to learn what they want, do what they want, and nobody would be allowed to put them away, either. Too bad I couldn't do anything now. After all, I was only eleven years old. Nobody listens to kids. I went back to my homework and finally finished the math and did some more work on my black-history report. As I looked through the black-history book and remembered what I learned in school, a plan began to form in my mind.

Once, Mrs. Stone showed us pictures of people during the civil-rights movement, marching with picket signs to protest against discrimination. Even in this book, there were pictures of people boycotting a coffee shop, a five-and-dime store, and a bus company. Eventually, their protests made a difference, and they got what they wanted. Now there were laws against that kind of discrimination. In some of the pictures, I noticed girls and boys my age, and some even younger. Maybe I could do something now and not wait until I was grown up.

If it is possible to boycott big companies and the

government, it is surely possible to boycott a grandfather who puts his grandson away. With everybody against Mr. Treadwell, he would have to bring T.J. home.

The more I thought of it, the more convinced I was that I had found the right solution. The next morning, I would start rounding up T.J.'s friends. But first I went into Billy's room to get his help.

The Boycott

———— ⊙ ⊙ ————

"HOW DO YOU boycott a person?" Billy asked, carefully setting a train car down on the track.

"March up and down in front of Mr. Treadwell's building, carrying signs and chanting."

He gave me a that's-the-dumbest-thing-I've-ever-heard look.

I slid over to sit closer to him. "It'll work. I'm sure of it. Mr. Treadwell's not made of stone. He must have feelings, and when he sees a bunch of people in front of his building telling him he was wrong for putting T.J. in a home, he'll have to take T.J. out. Don't you think that makes sense?"

"I think you're going to get into trouble."

"How?"

"Ma. She won't like it."

"Are you going to squeal on me?" When he didn't answer, I got to my feet and said. "Thanks—for nothing."

As I was leaving, he called, "Since when do you care so much about T.J.?"

"Since I realized *he* was not the real dope around here." With that, I slammed his door. No matter what Billy said, I was sure that a boycott would force Mr. Treadwell to bring T.J. home.

Wednesday was a bright, sunny day. By eight-fifteen, the schoolyard was full of kids playing ball, jumping rope, or just standing in groups, talking. The first people I decided to ask were Randy and Greg. They were playing a game of catch in the schoolyard but stopped to listen to me. I explained what had happened to T.J. and how we could bring him home.

"How do you know so much?" Randy asked.

I waggled my hand. "Never mind. The main thing is, I know. And my plan is a cinch to work," I said. "Once we boycott Mr. Treadwell, his friends will probably refuse to talk to him anymore. Everybody in church will give him dirty looks. The whole world will be against him. And he'll feel guilty for what he did."

"That's your plan?" Randy asked doubtfully.

"Sounds wack-o," said Greg. He nudged Randy. "Come on, let's play ball."

"Mr. Treadwell is wrong to have locked T.J. up," I said. "I don't know why he did it, but we have to do something to help T.J."

"Count me out," said Greg.

"Randy, you'll do it. Won't you?"

"We could get arrested."

"We have a right to protest," I said. "It's in the Constitution."

"Where?" Greg asked.

"It's an amendment."

"Can't fight City Hall."

"We're not fighting City Hall," I shouted. "And we can do that, too, if we want to."

"No dice," Greg said.

With a snap of his fingers, Randy said, "Anyway, we have baseball practice this afternoon."

"Big deal," I said.

"That's right. It is." They continued their game.

"Knuckleheads," I muttered as I walked away.

I might have expected that from Greg, but not from Randy. After all, he and T.J. were best friends. I told other friends of T.J.'s my plan and warned them not to tell any grownups. Some walked away without answering. Other kids asked too many questions, like how come I knew so much about T.J.'s being sent away, why he was sent away, and stuff like that.

"My mother knows his grandfather. Plus we go to the same church," I told them, leaving out the part about the roll book. That didn't help, though. Everyone was still afraid of getting into trouble or thought my idea was dumb, but then, they didn't know all the facts, and that's how it had to be.

The only person left to ask was Claudia. I waited until later that morning when Patricia went on an errand. She would never do anything to help T.J. and would probably talk Claudia into going along with her.

Claudia was in the back of the room, stapling a set of work sheets together for Mrs. Stone. This was the perfect time to get her on my side.

She smiled at me. "I got baby-doll pajamas for the slumber party. They're so cute. Little pink valentines all over them. We're going to have so much fun, Barbra."

"I'm getting mine soon," I said, even though I wasn't sure I was going to the party. Ma was really sticking to her word. She checked my homework and tests and even talked some more with Mrs. Stone.

In a low voice, I told Claudia my plan, while keeping an eye on Mrs. Stone, who was working with Angie and Carlos at her desk. When I finished, Claudia gave me a stare the same as Billy, Randy, and Greg had.

"It's for a good cause," I said, hoping all she needed was a little persuasion.

She sucked on her braces. "You asked Patricia?"

"I thought maybe you and I could do this together. Like we used to?"

She thought about it, then asked, "Who else is doing it?"

"How come you always care what everybody else is doing? Ever since Patricia moved here, you stick to her like glue. Don't you have a mind of your own?"

Claudia whispered, "I have a mind. And I don't want to do it."

Looking up from her desk, Mrs. Stone told me to sit down.

"Suppose Patricia says okay?" I asked quickly.

"You're going to ask her?"

It sounded like a dare. In a way, it was. Patricia never liked T.J. She would probably boycott to keep him locked up forever.

"Barbra," said Mrs. Stone in her warning voice.

"Forget it," I said to Claudia and took my seat.

At lunchtime, I went into the yard and sat on the cold stone steps, my chin cupped in my hands.

Kim sat down beside me. "I heard about your boycott," she said.

I felt like telling her what an eavesdropper she was, but was too disgusted to bother.

"I'll do it," she said.

"I changed my mind," I said, just to quiet her. I got up to go, then turned around. "Thanks for not telling Mrs. Stone on me."

. . .

Though I was disappointed that no one except Kim wanted to boycott with me, on the way home that afternoon, I decided to do it by myself. A protest of one was better than a protest of none. When I got home, I made my sign on easel paper. It was flimsy paper, but it was a large sheet. I wrote in big black capitals:

BE FAIR
BRING T.J. HOME
NOW!

Billy's door was slightly open. Through the crack, I saw him doing his homework at his desk. I sneaked downstairs to the kitchen and called Mr. Treadwell, hoping he wasn't home. The phone rang and rang. So far, everything was going fine. With the folded sign tucked under my jacket, I left the house.

I waited such a long time in front of Mr. Tread-well's building that I was beginning to think he was upstairs in his apartment after all and was going to stay there for the rest of the day. Even so, I continued to wait.

The block was fairly crowded with people, mostly kids. Some girls were jumping rope. A group of kids were playing punchball in the middle of the street. Two elderly men stood on the stoop next door, talking. No one had even an inkling of what was about to happen.

The only trouble was, the longer I waited, the more I wondered about what I was doing. Maybe this was a dumb thing to do. Boycotting Mr. Treadwell! Why should he listen to me? I felt like tearing up the sign and going back home, but then Kim came running up the block.

She carried a sign made of oaktag. A stick was glued to the back of it, making it look professional:

FIGHT CRUELTY
DOWN WITH MR. TREADWELL

"What are you doing here?" I asked.

"You're right about T.J. I'm boycotting, too."

"No. Go home."

She shook her head. "I want to stay. T.J.'s the nicest boy in the class."

Kim began marching up and down, chanting the words on my sign. For a moment, I just looked at her like she was crazy. But she didn't care. She kept marching.

Kids ran up the block to watch her. It was hard to believe that whiny voice of hers could be so powerful. After a while, I started chanting, too. At first my voice was low and shaky. Little kids started copying what we did and jumped around as if it was a game. A woman from a second-floor window tried to shoo us away, but we ignored her.

"Bring T.J. home!" we shouted. "Bring him home now!"

106

Kim jabbed her sign in the air like a majorette in a marching band. She got so carried away that when Mr. Treadwell appeared, I had to elbow her to get her attention.

Mr. Treadwell's beady black eyes blazed with anger. Everyone watched silently. More windows went up. It was so quiet that I could hear my heart pounding in my ears. I just stood there, feeling stupid.

Pretty soon, a teenage boy came out of Mr. Treadwell's building. "What's going on here?" he asked.

A snaggle-toothed kid took his fingers out of his mouth long enough to say, "It's about somebody named T.J." He pointed to Kim and said, "Ask her about it."

"Yeah," another boy said, hopping onto the hood of a parked car. "She's the ringleader."

"Not me. Barbra is," Kim said proudly and pushed me out in front of her.

Mr. Treadwell's eyes focused on me. It seemed as though he was noticing me for the first time. By the way he narrowed his eyes, I could tell he recognized me as the girl who sat in front of him in church, Ellen Conway's daughter. His mouth opened as if he wanted to say something, but no words came out.

"Still out there?" the woman said from the second-floor window. "Get away from my window, or I'll fix you but good." When no one paid any attention to her, she went back inside.

Mr. Treadwell stamped his cane. His nostrils flared. In a tight, angry voice, he said, "Stop acting foolish."

A man on the stoop said knowingly, "The police'll come and put an end to all this, Ezekiel. Don't worry."

"Is that what you did to T.J.?" I asked. "Sicced the police on him? He's only twelve years old and you put him away."

"That's cruel," said a girl wearing gold hoop earrings.

A woman walked past, shaking her head disapprovingly, and said, "Kids," like it was a dirty word.

I didn't care what the grownups thought. They couldn't stop me, and nobody really tried. So, with all my might, I began shouting, "Bring T.J. home. Bring him home now."

Mr. Treadwell snatched my sign from me and tore it to pieces. He stared at me a long time. I thought he was going to hit me, but he only turned and hobbled up the stoop, coughing and holding on to the railing.

"You can run, but you sure can't hide," the girl with the earrings called out.

"Right on!" someone else said.

Mr. Treadwell glanced over his shoulder at me. His words came out hoarse and crackly. "You don't know everything."

For some reason, those few words made me feel funny for being there and shouting at him. What didn't I know? Why didn't he tell me? I wanted to ask him, but he disappeared into his building. There was something so pitifully sad about Mr. Treadwell's limping down that long, dark hall.

Finally it was over, and I was glad. I started to leave, but not before that second-floor woman shouted, "Here's your right on," and dashed a bucket of ice-cold water down on us.

Confessions

———— o o ————

"YOU'RE ALL WET," Billy said when I came into the house.

Cold and shivering, I rushed upstairs to change. While I was brushing my hair, he came into my room.

"It was a bust. Wasn't it?"

"I feel bad enough. So leave me alone."

"When Ma comes home . . ."

"Don't you dare say a word."

For a while, I stayed in my room and did my homework. Afterwards I watched reruns of *Good Times* and *The Brady Bunch*, trying to forget everything.

When suppertime came, I didn't feel much like eating but forced my food down. I even ate all my spinach. But nothing I did helped. The memory of Mr. Treadwell limping up the stairs haunted me, even making it impossible to keep my mind on *The Peppermint Pig*. I wondered if our shouting gave him an asthma attack. With T.J. gone, who was taking care of him, getting his medicine if he needed it? All I wanted was for him to bring T.J. home. I didn't want to make him sick. But a picture of Mr. Treadwell, sick and alone in his apartment, stayed in my head.

Despite how scared I was, I couldn't keep this from Ma any longer. I stood in the doorway of the kitchen, watching her unload the dishwasher. With her back to me, I blurted out everything—starting with the protest, and working my way back to the roll book. I started crying.

Ma turned slowly as if stunned. "I don't believe what I'm hearing."

"I was trying to help." I wiped my runny nose on my sleeve. "I got mad because Mr. Treadwell was being so secretive, and because he lied. T.J.'s not with relatives."

"I am shocked, Barbra. How could you?"

"Me? But, Ma . . . Mr. Treadwell's the one who lied."

"That doesn't excuse what *you* did. Picketing in front of his building. He must've been devastated."

"But I was worried about T.J."

"And to show you care, you cause a bunch of people to shout things at an old man?"

I shrugged helplessly. "How else was I going to get Mr. Treadwell to admit what he did?"

"I'm sure there's more to it. You don't know exactly what happened or why Mr. Treadwell put T.J. away—if that's what he did."

"I'll call T.J. right now and prove it," I said, hoping I could get through to him this time.

"Hang up the phone," she said. She pinched the skin between her eyes, thinking.

"You got to understand," I pleaded.

She closed the dishwasher door. Undoing the strings of her apron, she said, "We'll talk about it later. Right now we're going to see Mr. Treadwell and apologize."

She took her coat from the closet, then handed me my jacket. When she noticed that it was still damp, she demanded an explanation. I told her about the bucket of water. She threw the wet jacket down on the Parsons table and handed me my blue down coat. It wasn't cold enough for that, but I knew better than to complain.

Ma walked the two blocks to Mr. Treadwell's with her hands in her pockets, looking straight ahead. In front of the building, pieces of my sign were plastered to the wet ground. I was scared to go up there.

"Ma?"

"Don't make it any harder," she said, without breaking her stride.

Mr. Treadwell didn't answer the bell the first time Ma rang. I crossed my fingers, wishing that nothing was wrong with him. After a minute the locks turned, and he stood before us in his plaid bathrobe and slippers. He looked from Ma to me and held his glance on me.

"Barbra has something to say to you," Ma said. "May we come in?"

He stepped aside and we came into the hot, stuffy apartment. A strong medicine smell filled the air. He moved a newspaper from the plastic-covered sofa so that we could sit.

Mr. Treadwell sat opposite us, looking smug. Suddenly I didn't feel sorry for him anymore. Besides, he was breathing fine now. All that raspy breathing must have been a put-on.

Ma cleared her throat and said, "Barbra?"

I was going to apologize, but instead I said, "I boycotted you because I thought it would make you bring T.J. home."

Ma gave me a stern look. When I still did not apologize, she said, "Barbra, my patience is . . ."

Mr. Treadwell put up his hand and stopped Ma in midsentence. It was as if we were both children in Mr. Treadwell's presence.

"Don't need no apology. Got truth on my side."

"How can you say that?" I blurted. "T.J.'s not with relatives. He's in a home." Ma shook me, but it was too late.

"Leave her be," Mr. Treadwell told Ma. To me he said, "You're only a child. You know less than you think. Like T.J., you can't see your nose for your face. What you did bothered me 'cause I don't like my business in the street. Now it don't much matter."

I moved closer to Ma, hoping for comfort, but she didn't put her arms around me. She let Mr. Treadwell talk to me in his crazy old way.

"You talk about what I did to him? What about what I did *for* him? I raise that boy, put clothes on his back and food in his mouth. His mother ran off on a crazy dream, but I'm the one here." He sputtered. "Put him away, indeed. My own flesh and blood. He took it on himself to go to that fool place, and I won't beg him to come home. He knows the way."

Ma finally spoke up. "Why? Why would T.J. run away?"

"T.J.'s like his mother, hates hearing the truth."

I knew what Mr. Treadwell was talking about. He meant the truth about T.J.'s mother becoming a big success and sending for him.

"Truth can be a hurting thing," he said, "if you're not ready for it." Just then, the tea kettle whistled, and Mr. Treadwell pulled himself to his feet. From the kitchen cupboard, he took down teacups and saucers.

"We're putting you through too much trouble," Ma said.

"It's cold out. Hot tea'll warm you up." He set out

114

milk, sugar, and a box of Tetley tea bags. After he put tea bags into a teapot, he added boiling water.

"At least let me help," Ma said, moving beside him.

"I'm strong and able."

While I sipped my creamy, sweet tea, Mr. Treadwell glanced at me and caught me staring. He wasn't the mean old man sitting stony-faced behind me in church. He loved T.J., who had run away from him. In his dark eyes I believed I could see the hurt he must be feeling. And what I had done made the hurt even worse.

"I'm sorry, Mr. Treadwell, for everything."

He mumbled what sounded like "Me, too."

After we finished the pot of tea, we got ready to leave. Mr. Treadwell offered to make some more, but Ma said we really had to go home now. "And if you need anything," Ma said, "call me."

"I manage just fine," he said, then added, "Thank you." He closed and locked the door behind us.

When we got home, almost an hour later, Billy started pumping me with questions.

"I apologized," I said simply. "I can't believe how wrong I was."

I was about to tell him the rest when Ma came into the kitchen and told him she had to talk privately to me.

On the table she set a small jar of colored beads. She pulled out a kitchen chair and said, "Sit."

"You're corn-braiding my hair now?" I asked as she began undoing my two thick braids.

"I thought you wanted your hair braided."

"It's so late," I said, squirming.

"I feel like doing it now. Be still."

"Because of what happened at Mr. Treadwell's?" I asked, even though that reason really made no sense. Without answering, she parted my hair and began braiding beads into a small section. She pulled so tight I was sure she was still angry at me. But why would she be giving me something I've wanted for a long time if she was still angry? The way Ma was acting confused me.

I ran my fingers over the tiny, smooth beads woven into my braids. "Wait till everybody gets a load of me."

She seemed too deep in thought to answer me.

Even with the mess I had made, I believed there was still one last chance to set things right. "Ma, take me to see T.J."

"I don't think so. We've meddled enough."

"But if he only knew how his grandfather really feels. You saw how sad Mr. Treadwell was. I bet T.J. is sad, too. I can fix everything, Ma. Let me try."

Ma tilted my head up. She smiled slightly. "You're just like Daddy."

"What?"

116

"When he believed in something, he stuck to it. Right or wrong. I saw that in you tonight."

"Me? Like Daddy?" I was really surprised. "He was so smart and everything."

"A little trouble in school doesn't mean you're not smart."

While Ma braided, I thought about Daddy and how he gave me piggyback rides around the house and how he read his newspaper articles to me.

"In fact, when Daddy was a boy, he had trouble in math," Ma said. "Multiplication, I think."

"You never told me."

"I wanted to. Grandma said Daddy used to make excuses. Since math came hard for Grandpa, Daddy claimed that to be a poor math student was in his genes."

"Maybe it is," I said.

"Sure. No wonder Mrs. Stone started writing nice comments on your assignments. Bad genes, indeed."

Although I laughed along with Ma, her mentioning my teacher reminded me of something serious. "Ma, do I have to tell Mrs. Stone about the roll book?"

"I'll leave that up to you."

She probably expected me to confess to Mrs. Stone, but I wasn't that brave. I didn't think I could tell her, at least not while I was still in her class. When

I got to junior high school, maybe I would come back and do it.

My scalp felt as if it were being pulled off, but I didn't complain. I was just glad Ma was near me and telling me things about Daddy. When she was finished, it was almost ten-thirty. Billy had long since gone to bed. Ma held a mirror in front of my face.

"They're beautiful." I twisted my head from side to side, and the beads clicked.

"Saturday night, you'll be the prettiest girl at the slumber party."

"I can go? What about the punishment?"

"I promised you could go if you improved your math. You have."

I hugged her tight. "You're the best, Ma."

"About your boycott . . ." She pulled me away. "I want you to be independent, to care about people . . . I believe that you meant well, but you didn't have all the facts, and besides which . . ."

"You're going to punish me."

"Some things, Barbra, can't be wiped clean by staying in the house for a few weeks. I don't ever want you to stop caring about people and having beliefs, but I do want you to come and talk to me before you go off on some wild idea. I won't always agree, but I will listen and hope you'll listen, too."

She touched my cheek and said, "Get ready for bed. I'll be up after a while."

As I put on my pajamas, I heard Ma sweeping the kitchen floor. Then she turned out the lights and came upstairs.

She sat down on the bed next to me and tied a silky kind of scarf around my head to make sleeping on the beads easier.

I slid down under the covers. Ma kissed me good night and turned out my light.

I lay in bed listening to the swish of traffic on the Drive and thinking how getting punished is a whole lot easier. At least, when the punishment is over, everything is fine. This way, I'd have to think about what I did for a long, long time.

Fresh Starts

———— o o ————

ON THURSDAY, it was pouring rain. I put on a rain hat to keep my braids from getting soaked and hurried to school.

Two little boys splashed through the puddles covering the yard. All the fifth- and sixth-graders were milling around the indoor line-up area at the right of the main lobby.

I was about to go inside when I heard Kim call, "Wait up."

She ran toward me in her yellow slicker with matching hat and umbrella. But just as she reached me, Patricia and Claudia came up behind me. Suddenly I was in between Kim and my friends and felt jittery.

"Your hair!" Patricia screeched.

"You look funny," said Claudia.

I got a sick, queer feeling. "What do you mean—funny?" I asked.

120

Claudia hunched her shoulders and said, "At least, they're not permanent. You can always change them."

"Change . . ."

"I think they're beautiful," said Kim.

Patricia walked around me like I was a statue on display. She snapped her fingers. "They're just what the club needs. They can be our trademark."

Patricia turned to Kim as if remembering that she was standing there among us. I prayed that she wouldn't say anything mean to Kim. Luckily, Kim had disappeared into the crowd. I was relieved for several reasons: Kim was gone, she hadn't mentioned the boycott, and Patricia didn't say anything about her.

We went into the girls' bathroom across the lobby and we had our first official club meeting. Although it was a great feeling to be part of everything, it bothered me that Patricia wanted to copy my braids. One of the reasons I liked them was they were different. Yet I was so thrilled to be off punishment and going to the party that I didn't make a fuss about it. Now and then, as I wrote down things we said, I shook my head because I loved the clicking sound the beads made.

Our meeting was interrupted by the line-up whistle. When we got in line to go into our classroom, Randy said, "Here come the three stooges." That didn't bother me, though.

Everything was going fine until art class. I was rummaging through the supply closet, searching for a box of pastels, when Kim came up behind me and tapped me on the shoulder.

"Did your mother get mad about your wet clothes?" she whispered. "My mother was so mad at me."

Patricia was gazing curiously at me.

"Later, Kim," I said. Even though I wanted to talk to her, I made a beeline back to where I was sitting with Patricia and Claudia.

"What did she want?" Patricia asked.

"Oh, you know Kim."

I got busy with my still-life drawing, afraid to look up and see Kim staring at me wide-eyed and hurt. I felt like such an idiot for being scared to talk to Kim. She had helped me when no one else would. It was only fair she should know how our boycott turned out. Besides, there was nothing so horrible about her, anyway.

Near the end of the period, when everyone was cleaning up, I made a decision. I passed a note to Kim. But it never made it to her desk. Randy, instead of passing the note on when it reached him, opened it. I jumped up to stop him, and Mrs. Rinquist broke in.

After reading the note, she said, "Kim, Barbra wants you to call her after school. It's important." She tore up the note and tossed it into the wastepaper basket. "Pack your belongings, people, and line up."

Trying to be invisible, I gathered my books and supplies and walked to the line, keeping my head down.

On the way downstairs, Patricia cornered me on the landing. "Why were you writing notes to fat Gumdrop?" she said loud enough for Kim to hear.

Claudia said, "I bet she's the mystery friend."

"Gumdrop?" Patricia shrieked. "Be serious. Who'd have that . . ." She looked me straight in the eye. "Is fatso the mystery friend?"

"Don't call her names," I said.

"She's even sticking up for her," Patricia said.

"Well, what did Kim ever do to you, anyway?"

Claudia began to giggle.

Patricia asked, "Did she give you a bag of gumdrops to be her friend?"

They howled with laughter. I was shaking Claudia's arm to get her to stop when I saw Kim darting back up the stairs away from the class. This was so unfair, and I was stupid for putting up with it. Before Patricia moved into the neighborhood, I wasn't this way, afraid to talk to anybody I pleased. What was so great about Patricia, anyway? Her red-and-white room? Her VCR? Her nice clothes? Her club?

Patricia linked her arm through mine. "I was only joking around. I know Kim isn't the mystery friend."

"You're right," I said, pulling my arm from hers. "Kim isn't my mystery friend. She's my friend. Period."

Patricia snorted. "Well, any friend of a gumdrop is no friend of mine. I'm not having gumdrops or friends of gumdrops at my party or in my club." With that, she strode off.

Claudia put her arm on mine. "She'll change her mind. You'll see."

"I don't care," I said, but I did care—a whole lot. I'd waited so long for this party, and now I was going to be left out. No matter what Claudia said, I knew better. When Patricia made up her mind to dislike someone, she never changed.

"Claudia, you coming or not?" Patricia called.

I tried to swallow the thickness building in my throat and said, "Claudia, since you don't have ballet today, why not walk home with me—like we used to?"

"Then she'll be mad at me, too," Claudia said.

"So?"

"But she's my best friend." And she ran to catch up to Patricia.

As I walked home alone, tears sprang to my eyes. I tried sniffing them back, but they came anyway.

With no place to go and nothing to do, I slouched into the kitchen Saturday and plopped down at the table. Billy had already gone to his baseball practice.

I called Kim, but she wasn't home. Ma was cleaning out the refrigerator.

"When I'm through with this, we can go for your pj's." She uncovered a plastic container. "Peew!" She dumped the green, moldy food into the sink.

Fingering the fruit in the bowl on the table, I said, "I'm not going."

"What do you mean? You've been looking forward to that party for so long." She closed the refrigerator.

"Patricia hates Kim, and I stuck up for her."

"You did the right thing," she said, after I explained the whole situation.

"Finally. But now they kicked me out of the club, and I don't have any friends."

"Meaning Patricia." Ma sat down beside me. "To be honest, she doesn't sound like much of a friend. But what about Claudia? You two used to be close."

"Not anymore."

"Well, Kim sounds nice enough."

"She is, but she—I can't explain it."

A while later, I was watching cartoons on the living room TV when Ma came inside. "I was just thinking," she said, "since I don't have any plans this afternoon and neither do you . . ."

"I don't feel like going to a movie." I folded my arms across my chest and stared at the TV screen, not really paying attention.

"I was thinking that we might go visit T.J."

I nearly knocked over the ottoman, getting up. "You mean it? I don't get it. Before, you said . . ."

"Why shouldn't you visit him?"

"No reason. Can we go now? I'm all ready." She took off her apron and hung it up. "I'll call and arrange it."

Then I remembered the visiting-hour schedule. "Ma, we can't go until four o'clock."

"That gives us plenty of time to have brunch. You choose the restaurant."

I suspected the reason Ma suggested the visit was that she was feeling sorry for me. It was as though she was trying to make up for my missing the slumber party, but nothing could do that.

When we got to Redding, we met the director, Paula Jamison. She went with us to the lounge, where we waited for T.J. Ms. Jamison and Ma talked about their families and their jobs.

I wished T.J. would hurry up. He finally walked into the room. I think he was happy to see me because he had a broad smile on his face.

"Anthony Jordan Brodie, why didn't you call me?" I demanded.

He shrugged and acted embarrassed. Ma hugged him and said how glad she was to see him.

"T.J., why don't you show Barbra around?" Ms. Jamsion said.

Ma and Ms. Jamison stayed in the waiting room.

T.J. and I went upstairs. I didn't really want to see this place. I was afraid a home for orphans and unwanted kids would be dreary.

We went into the library. Lumpy chairs were clustered in front of a fireplace, which T.J. said was fake. Tables were scattered around the room, and along one wall were shelves of books: the *Little House* series, *Robinson Crusoe*, *Treasure Island*, *Little Women*. There were no books by Nina Bawden, but there were some by E. B. White and Mildred Taylor.

"It's a nice library," I said.

"Yeah, but hardly anyone uses it."

As we walked through the hallway, the floorboards under the carpet creaked. "Where is everybody?" I said in a whisper.

"Watching TV, I guess, playing Ping-Pong in the basement, or in the back yard. It's like home. We all get chores to do."

"Only it isn't home," I meant to say to myself but said out loud. To cover up, I asked him if he heard about the boycott.

He nodded but didn't say who told him. His grandfather? I wondered.

"It was a stupid thing to do," I said. "I must've been temporarily insane or something."

"It doesn't matter." He pushed open a set of double doors to the dining room. Thin white curtains flapped at the opened window. Someone was playing ball outside. Steamy tomato and beef smells came from the kitchen, just off the dining room. T.J. began setting the table.

"I started to call you once to thank you for the letter and cookies," he said. "But I was kind of mixed up. I didn't want to talk to anybody, or have to answer a lot of questions. I . . . It's hard to put into words. But . . ."

"I know what you mean."

He smiled as if thankful for not having to explain his feelings. Finally I asked him about going home. T.J. put the forks next to each plate without answering.

"Your grandfather misses you." I followed him around the table.

"I don't want to talk about him."

"Why not?"

He stubbornly changed the subject. "What's with the braids? You look like an Egyptian princess."

"Why won't you go home? That's where you belong."

He looked past me and said, "I like it here. In school, we're doing geometry. The teacher gives us contracts. So we work on our own."

"But your grandfather loves you."

He rammed a chair into the table and stalked into the hallway. I sat down next to him on the steps. I wanted to tell him that running away from problems never solved anything. But who was I to talk?

Scratching at a torn piece of the faded wallpaper, he said, "You know how I ended up here? Pop said a lot of mean things about my mother. I ran down in the subway. It was real late. A policeman started asking me a bunch of questions like what was wrong, where I lived, where were my parents. I told him I wasn't going back. Not ever. And I wouldn't give him my address. At first, I stayed a couple of days in this other place, not as nice as here. I can live here as long as I want to."

"You're stubborn, just like him. Your grandfather made tea for my mother and me. You know what I found out? He wants you to come back. He even said so." I crossed my fingers and hoped God wouldn't strike me down dead for lying.

He was quiet a long time, then said, as if telling me a secret, "That Friday, the day we went to the bookstore . . . well, later, I called my mother. She promised she was going to send for me real soon. When I hung up, I told Pop that. But *he* said that she was only thinking about her singing and not about me. 'You're my responsibility now,' he said, like I was a big burden or something." Shredding the piece of wallpaper, he said, "So I'm going to stay here until she sends for me. That'll show him."

"Suppose your grandfather is right and you're wrong?"

He looked at me angrily. "Go on. Take his side."

"I'm not. It's just . . ."

"I'm staying. I have a real nice room. We even have color TV."

I knew I should shut up, but I couldn't help myself. "Don't tell me you prefer color TV to your grandfather, your own flesh and blood?" I felt like crying. "Your grandfather misses you." I miss you, I wanted to say.

He closed his eyes. "I can't go home."

"Yes. You can."

He scrubbed his foot against the step. He seemed so frightened and lonely in a way I had never seen before.

"I'll walk you downstairs," he said.

Just before we reached the waiting room, he touched my arm. "Wait. I have to tell you something." First he looked down at his feet, then directly at me. "Remember when I first became your tutor? It was because I asked Mrs. Stone to let me. I wanted you to know that."

"You rat!" I said happily.

Not too long ago, I was wishing T.J. lived on another planet. And now . . . In such a short time, everything had changed. I watched him run up the stairs, then disappear out of sight.

"Did you have a good visit?" Ma asked as we walked to the subway.

"He won't go home, Ma. I think he wants to, and Mr. Treadwell wants him back. It doesn't make sense."

She took my hand. "He probably needs time to sort things out."

On the subway ride downtown, I thought about T.J., Claudia, Patricia, Kim, me. My biggest problems, my math grade, and my friends deserting me, were nothing compared to T.J.'s, which was his mother, and that was a terrible thing. How alone he must be feeling! I was scared for T.J. because he trusted his mother so much. I also felt guilty, because even though my problems were small, they felt big.

Monday morning, Claudia, Patricia, and other girls from my class were clustered together in a corner of the schoolyard. I walked over.

Patricia said, "Club meetings are private." After that, they all walked away, and an achy lump got caught in my throat.

The hurting feeling stayed with me after I went into the classroom. It seemed that almost every girl in the class was wearing a Red-Hot Ladies shirt, jeans, and red sneakers. They all had red hair clips in their hair. Once Patricia and Angie paraded in front of my desk, modeling their outfits. A while later, Claudia came over to borrow a pencil and told me how great the slumber party was.

"But I missed you," she said.

Listening to her made me wish I was still a Red-Hot Lady. If I were in the club, I would share their jokes and secrets, and dress like them. But then I thought about something.

Looking like them, acting like them, and doing what they did meant I couldn't be me. I ran my fingers through my braids. The beads were cool and smooth to my touch. Did I really look like an Egyptian princess, like T.J. said? Probably not. I just looked like me, and that was good enough. I smiled to myself. Patricia won't try to boss me around anymore. And even if she did, I wouldn't let her.

"This will be our last lesson in black history," said Mrs. Stone.

Sighs of relief turned to groans when she added, "I'll expect your reports tomorrow. Today we'll be reading and discussing poetry."

Since we had already learned about the civil-rights movement, slavery, abolitionists, and reconstruction, she said she would tell us about a time not too many children know about.

"It was called the Harlem Renaissance, during the 1920s. It was a reckless, wild time in this country. People were dancing the Charleston."

I was shocked when she demonstrated the dance, kicking her legs up. "There was prohibition against selling liquor. Nevertheless, people broke the law and made a concoction called bathtub gin."

"Must've been some dirty gin," Randy called out. Everyone laughed.

132

Mrs. Stone didn't scold him for calling out. "I suspect you're right. It wasn't all fun, however."

The lesson turned out to be the best one we had, because Mrs. Stone read the poetry as if she were acting different parts in a play. She was so good I wondered if she had ever been an actress. She read poems by Countee Cullen, whom the library on 136th Street was named after, and Alice Dunbar-Nelson and Langston Hughes.

" 'What happens to a dream deferred?' " she recited. " 'Does it dry up like a raisin in the sun? / Or fester like a sore—' "

I was so caught up in listening to Mrs. Stone, I didn't even notice when the door opened and someone came into the room. It was Randy who called out and made me look toward the door.

I could hardly believe it. T.J. was back, standing in front of the room. He nervously adjusted his knapsack on his shoulder like a new kid just entering the class. T.J. was not a stranger, though, and at once everyone started shouting at him.

Mrs. Stone held up her hand. "Contain yourselves. You may welcome Anthony back after the lesson." She took the note he'd brought from the office. "Hang up your jacket," she told him. She made it seem as if he'd only been absent for two days. He took his usual seat beside me and began putting his things into his desk.

"I want you to listen to some music." Mrs. Stone showed us an album called '*Nuff Said*, recorded by a singer named Nina Simone. "While you listen," she said, carefully taking the record from its jacket, "write your feelings about the poems, songs, lessons, everything we've been studying in black history. Afterwards, you'll share what you wrote."

She put the record on, and the singer's voice made me think of T.J.'s mother. I glanced at T.J. He looked at me.

"How come you changed your mind about coming home?" I whispered.

Before he could answer, Mrs. Stone said, above the music, "Barbra, I hope your conversation is more important than my lesson."

"No, ma'am," I said.

"Then get to work. I gave an assignment."

"Um, Mrs. Stone, I need paper," T.J. said. "And my pen is out of ink."

"Barbra, lend him a pen and some paper."

Along with the paper and pen, I slipped a note to him that said: "I bet the only reason you came back was to bug me. Right?"

He wrote: "RIGHT!"

Even though I crumpled up the note and threw it into his lap, it felt good passing notes to T.J. again. I turned my notebook to a clean page and began the assignment.